Charles Egbert Craddock

The young mountaineers

Charles Egbert Craddock

The young mountaineers

ISBN/EAN: 9783743358713

Manufactured in Europe, USA, Canada, Australia, Japa

Cover: Foto ©Andreas Hilbeck / pixelio.de

Manufactured and distributed by brebook publishing software (www.brebook.com)

Charles Egbert Craddock

The young mountaineers

HE WAS PALLID AND PANTING (see page 221)

THE YOUNG MOUNTAINEERS

SHORT STORIES

BY

CHARLES EGBERT CRADDOCK

WITH ILLUSTRATIONS BY
MALCOLM FRASER

BOSTON AND NEW YORK
HOUGHTON, MIFFLIN AND COMPANY
The Riverside Press, Cambridge
1897

The Riverside Press, Cambridge, Mass., U. S. A.
Electrotyped and Printed by H. O. Houghton and Company.

CONTENTS

		PAGE
THE MYSTERY OF OLD DADDY'S WINDOW	. .	1
'WAY DOWN IN POOR VALLEY	. . . .	26
A MOUNTAIN STORM	. . . .	63
BORROWING A HAMMER	. . . . . .	83
THE CONSCRIPTS' HOLLOW	. . . . . .	103
A WARNING	. . . .	172
AMONG THE CLIFFS	. . . .	186
IN THE "CHINKING"	. . . . . .	208
ON A HIGHER LEVEL	. . . . . .	230
CHRISTMAS DAY ON OLD WINDY MOUNTAIN	.	245

LIST OF ILLUSTRATIONS

PAGE

HE WAS PALLID AND PANTING (see page 221) *Frontispiece.*

TOGETHER THEY WENT OVER THE CLIFF . . . 48

HOW LONG WAS IT TO LAST 190

IN THE MIDST OF THE TORRENT 242

THE MYSTERY OF OLD DADDY'S WINDOW

PICTURE to yourself a wild ravine, gashing a mountain spur, and with here and there in its course abrupt descents. One of these is so deep and sheer that it might be called a precipice.

High above it, from the steep slope on either hand, beetling crags jut out. Their summits almost meet at one point, and thus the space below bears a rude resemblance to a huge window. Through it you might see the blue heights in the distance; or watch the clouds and sunshine shift over the sombre mountain across the narrow valley; or mark, after the day has faded, how the great Scorpio draws its shining curves along the dark sky.

One night Jonas Creyshaw sat alone in the porch of his log cabin, hard by on the slope of the ravine, smoking his pipe and gazing meditatively at " Old Daddy's Window." The moon was full, and its rays fell aslant on one of the cliffs, while the rugged face of the opposite crag was in the shadow.

Suddenly he became aware that something was moving about the precipice, the brink of which seems the sill of the window. Although this precipice is sheer and insurmountable, a dark figure had risen from it, and stood plainly defined against the cliff, which presented a comparatively smooth surface to the brilliant moonlight.

Was it a shadow? he asked himself hastily.

His eyes swept the ravine, only thirty feet wide at that point, which lies between the two crags whose jutting summits almost meet above it to form Old Daddy's Window.

There was no one visible to cast a shadow.

It seemed as if the figure had unaccountably emerged from the sheer depths below.

Only for a moment it stood motionless

against the cliff. Then it flung its arms wildly above its head, and with a nimble spring disappeared — upward.

Jonas Creyshaw watched it, his eyes distended, his face pallid, his pipe trembling in his shaking hand.

"Mirandy!" he quavered faintly.

His wife, a thin, ailing woman with pinched features and an uncertain eye, came to the door.

"Thar," he faltered, pointing with his pipe-stem — "jes' a minit ago — I seen it! — a ghost riz up over the bluff inter Old Daddy's Window!"

The woman fell instantly into a panic.

"'T war n't a-beckonin', war it? 'T war n't a-beckonin'? 'Kase ef it war, ye'll hev ter die right straight! That air a sure sign."

A little of Jonas Creyshaw's pluck and common sense came back to him at this unpleasant announcement.

"Not on *his* say-so," he stoutly averred. "I ain't a-goin' ter do the beck nor the bid of enny onmannerly harnt ez hev tuk up the

notion ter riz up over the bluff inter Old
Daddy's Window, an' sot hisself ter motionin'
ter me."

He rose hastily, knocked the ashes out of
his pipe, and followed his wife into the house.
There he paused abruptly.

The room was lighted by the fitful flicker
of the fire, for the nights were still chilly,
and an old man, almost decrepit, sat dozing
in his chair by the hearth.

" Mirandy," said Jonas Creyshaw in a
whisper, " 'pears like ter me ez father hed
better not be let ter know 'bout'n that thar
harnt. It mought skeer him so ez he could n't
live another minit. He hev aged some lately
— an' he air weakly."

This was " Old Daddy."

Before he had reached his thirtieth year,
he was thus known, far and wide.

" He air the man ez hev got a son," the
mountaineers used to say in grinning expla-
nation. " Ter hear him brag 'bout'n that thar
boy o' his'n, ye'd think he war the only man
in Tennessee ez ever hed a son."

Throughout all these years the name given in jocose banter had clung to him, and now, hallowed by ancient usage, it was accorded to him seriously, and had all the sonorous effect of a title.

So they said nothing to Old Daddy, but presently, when he had hobbled off to bed in the adjoining shed-room, they fell to discussing their terror of the apparition, and thus it chanced that the two boys, Tad and Si, first made, as it were, the ghost's acquaintance.

Tad, a stalwart fellow of seventeen, sat listening spellbound before the glowing embers. Si, a wiry, active, tow-headed boy of twelve, perched with dangling legs on a chest, and looked now at the group by the fire, and now through the open door at the brilliant moonlight.

" Waal, sir," he muttered, " I 'll hev ter gin up the notion o' gittin' that comical young ow*el*, what I hev done set my heart onto. 'Kase ef I war ter fool round Old Daddy's Window, *now*, whilst I war a-cotchin' o' the ow*el*, the ghost mought — cotch — *Me!*"

A sorry ghost, to be sure, that has nothing better to do than to "cotch" *him!* But perhaps Si Creyshaw is not the only one of us who has an inflated idea of his own importance.

He was greatly awed, and he found many suggestions of supernatural presence about the familiar room. As the fire alternately flared and faded, the warping-bars looked as if they were dancing a clumsy measure. The handle of a portly jug resembled an arm stuck akimbo, and its cork, tilted askew, was like a hat set on one side; Si fancied there was a most unpleasant grimace below that hat. The churn-dasher, left upon a shelf to dry, was sardonically staring him out of countenance with its half-dozen eyes. The strings of red pepper-pods and gourds and herbs, swinging from the rafters, rustled faintly; it sounded to Si like a moan.

He wished his father and mother would talk about some wholesome subject, like Spot's new calf, for instance, instead of whispering about the mystery of Old Daddy's Window.

He wished Tad would not look, as he listened, so much like a ghost himself, with his starting eyes and pale, intent face. He even wished that the baby would wake up, and put some life into things with a good healthy, rousing bawl.

But the baby slept peacefully on, and after so long a time Si Creyshaw slept too.

With broad daylight his courage revived. He was no longer afraid to think of the ghost. In fact, he experienced a pleased importance in giving Old Daddy a minute account of the wonderful apparition, for he *felt* as if he had seen it.

"'Pears ter me toler'ble comical, gran'dad, ez they never tole ye a word 'bout'n it all," he said in conclusion. "Ye mought hev liked ter seen the harnt. Ef he war 'quainted with ye when he lived in this life, he mought hev stopped an' jowed sociable fur a spell!"

How brave this small boy was in the cheerful sunshine!

Old Daddy hardly seemed impressed with the pleasure he had missed in losing a sociable "jow" with a ghostly crony. He sat silent, blinking in the sunshine that fell through the gourd-vines which clambered about the porch where Si had placed his chair.

"'T war n't much of a sizable sperit," Si declared; he seemed courageous enough now to measure the ghost like a tailor. "It war n't more 'n four feet high, ez nigh ez dad could jedge. Toler'ble small fur a harnt!"

Still the old man made no reply. His wrinkled hands were clasped on his stick. His white head, shaded by his limp black hat, was bent down close to them. There was a slow, pondering expression on his face, but an excited gleam in his eye. Presently, he pointed backward toward a little unhewn log shanty that served as a barn, and rising with unwonted alacrity, he said to the boy, —

"Fotch me the old beastis!"

Silas Creyshaw stood amazed, for Old Daddy had not mounted a horse for twenty years.

"Studyin' 'bout'n the harnt so much hev teched him in the head," the small boy concluded. Then he made an excuse, for he knew his grandfather was too old and feeble to safely undertake a solitary jaunt on horseback.

"I war tole not ter leave ye fur a minit, gran'dad. I war ter stay nigh ye an' mind yer bid."

"That's my bid!" said the old man sternly. "Fotch the beastis."

There was no one else about the place. Jonas Creyshaw had gone fishing shortly after daybreak. His wife had trudged off to her sister's house down in the cove, and had taken the baby with her. Tad was ploughing in the cornfield on the other side of the ravine. Si had no advice, and he had been brought up to think that Old Daddy's word was law.

When the old man, mounted at last, was jogging up the road, Tad chanced to come to the house for a bit of rope to mend the plough-gear. He saw, far up the leafy vista, the departing cavalier. He cast a look of amazed reproach upon Si. Then, speechless with astonishment, he silently pointed at the distant figure.

Si was a logician.

"I never lef' *him*," he said. "He lef' *me*."

"Ye oughter rej'ice in yer whole bones while ye hev got 'em," Tad returned, with withering sarcasm. "When dad kems home, some of 'em 'll git bruk, sure. War n't ye tole not ter leave him fur *nuthin'*, ye triflin' shoat!"

"He lef' *me!*" Si stoutly maintained.

Meantime, Old Daddy journeyed on.

Except for the wonderful mountain air, the settlement, three miles distant, had nothing about it to indicate its elevation. It was far from the cliffs, and there was no view. It was simply a little hollow of a clearing scooped out among the immense forests. When the mountaineers clear land, they do it effectually. Not a tree was left to embellish the yards of any of the four or five little log huts that constituted the hamlet, and the glare was intense.

As six or eight loungers sat smoking about

the door of the store, there was nothing to intercept their astonished view of Old Daddy when he suddenly appeared out of the gloomy forest, blinking in the sun and bent half double with fatigue.

Even the rudest and coarsest of these mountaineers accord a praiseworthy deference to the aged among them. Old Daddy was held in reverential estimation at home, and was well accustomed to the respect shown him now, when, for the first time in many years, he had chosen to jog abroad. They helped him to dismount, and carried him bodily into the store. After he had tilted his chair back against the rude counter, he looked around with an important face upon the attentive group.

"My son," shrilly piped out Old Daddy, — "my son air the strongest man ever seen, sence Samson!"

"I hev always hearn that sayin', Old Daddy," acquiesced an elderly codger, who, by reason of "rheumatics," made no pretension to muscle.

A gigantic young blacksmith looked down at his corded hammer-arm, but said nothing.

A fly — several flies — buzzed about the sorghum barrel.

"My son," shrilly piped out Old Daddy, —"my son air the bes' shot on this hyar mounting."

"That's a true word, Old Daddy," assented the schoolmaster, who had ceased to be a Nimrod since devoting himself to teaching the young idea how to shoot.

The hunters smoked in solemn silence.

The shadow of a cloud drifted along the bare sandy stretch of the clearing.

"My son," shrilly piped out Old Daddy, —"my son hev got the peartest boys in Tennessee."

"I'll gin ye that up, Old Daddy," cheerfully agreed the miller, whose family consisted of two small "daughters."

The fathers of other "peart boys" cleared their throats uneasily, but finally subsided without offering contradiction.

A jay-bird alighted on a blackberry bush

outside, fluttered all his blue and white feathers, screamed harshly, bobbed his crested head, and was off on his gay wings.

"My son," shrilly piped out Old Daddy, —"my son hev been gifted with the sight o' what no other man on this mounting hev ever viewed."

The group sat amazed, expectant. But the old man preserved a stately silence. Only when the storekeeper eagerly insisted, "What hev Jonas seen? what war he gin ter view?" did Old Daddy bring the fore legs of the chair down with a thump, lean forward, and mysteriously pipe out like a superannuated cricket, —

"My son, — my son hev seen a harnt, what riz up over the bluff a-purpose!"

"Whar 'bouts?" "When?" "Waal, sir!" arose in varied clamors.

So the proud old man told the story he had journeyed three laborious miles to spread. It had no terrors for him, so completely was fear swallowed up in admiration of his wonderful son, who had added to his other perfections the gift of seeing ghosts.

The men discussed it eagerly. There were some jokes cracked — as it was still broad noonday — and at one of these Old Daddy took great offense, more perhaps because the disrespect was offered to his son rather than to himself.

"Jes' gin Jonas the word from me," said the young blacksmith, meaning no harm and laughing good-naturedly, "ez I kin tell him percisely what makes him see harnts; it air drinkin' so much o' this onhealthy whiskey, what hain't got no tax paid onto it. I looks ter see him jes' a-staggerin' the nex' time I comes up with him."

Old Daddy rose with affronted dignity.

"My son," he declared vehemently, — "my son ain't gin over ter drinkin' whiskey, tax or no tax. An' he ain't got no call ter stagger — *like some folks!*"

And despite all apology and protest, he left the house in a huff.

His old bones ached with the unwonted exercise, and were rudely enough jarred by the rough roads and the awful gaits of his ancient

steed. The sun was hot, and so was his heart,
and when he reached home, infinitely fatigued
and querulous, he gave his son a sorry account
of his reception at the store. As he concluded, saying that five of the men had sent
word that they would be at Jonas Creyshaw's
house at moon-rise "ter holp him see the
harnt," his son's brow darkened, and he strode
heavily out of the room.

He usually exhibited in a high degree the
hospitality characteristic of these mountaineers, but now it had given way to a still
stronger instinct.

"Si," he said, coming suddenly upon the
boy, "put out right now fur Bently's store at
the settle*mint*, an' tell them sneaks ez hang
round thar ter sarch round thar own houses
fur harnts, ef they hanker ter see enny harnts.
Ef they hev got the insurance ter kem hyar,
they'll see wusser sights 'n enny harnts. Tell
'em I ain't a-goin' ter 'low no man ter cross
my doorstep ez don't show Old Daddy the
right medjure o' respec'. They'd better keep
out'n my way ginerally."

So with this bellicose message Si set out.
But an unlucky idea occurred to him as he
went plodding along the sandy road.

"Whilst I'm a-goin' on this hyar harnt's
yerrand"— The logical Si brought up with
a shiver.

"I went ter say—whilst I'm a-goin' on
this hyar yerrand fur the harnt"— This
was as bad.

"Whilst," he qualified once more, "I'm
a-goin' on this hyar yerrand *'bout'n* the harnt,
I mought ez well skeet off in them deep woods
a piece ter see ef enny wild cherries air ripe
on that tree by the spring. I'll hev plenty
o' time."

But even Si could not persuade himself that
the cherries were ripe, and he stood for a moment under the tree, staring disconsolately at
the distant blue ridges shimmering through
the heated air. The sunlight was motionless, languid; it seemed asleep. The drowsy
drone of insects filled the forest. As Si
threw himself down to rest on the rocky brink
of the mountain, a grasshopper sprang away

suddenly, high into the air, with an agility
that suggested to him the chorus of a song,
which he began to sing in a loud and self-
sufficient voice : —

> " The grasshopper said — ' Now, don't ye see
> Thar 's mighty few dancers sech ez me —
> Sech ez *me!* — Sech ez ME ! ' " —

This reminded Si of his own capabilities as
a dancer. He rose and began to caper nimbly,
executing a series of steps that were singularly
swift, spry, and unexpected, — a good deal on
the grasshopper's method. His tattered black
hat bobbed up and down on his tow head;
his brown jeans trousers, so loose on his lean
legs, flapped about hilariously; his bare heels
flew out right and left; he snapped his fingers to mark the time; now and then he stuck
his arms akimbo, and cut what he called the
" widgeon-ping." But his freckled face was
as grave as ever, and all the time that he
danced he sang : —

> " In the middle o' the night the rain kem down,
> An' gin the corn a fraish start out'n the ground,
> An' I thought nex' day ez I stood in the door,
> That sassy bug mus' be drownded sure !

But thar war Goggle-eyes, peart an' gay,
Twangin' an' a-tunin' up — 'Now, dance away !
Ye may sarch night an' day ez a constancy
An' ye won't find a fiddler sech ez me !
   Sech ez *me !* — Sech ez Me ! ' "

As he sank back exhausted upon the ground,
a new aspect of the scene caught his attention.

Those blue mountains were purpling —
there was an ever-deepening flush in the west.
It was close upon sunset, and while he had
wasted the time, the five men to whom his
father had sent that stern message forbidding
them to come to his house were perhaps on
their way thither, with every expectation of a
cordial welcome. There might be a row —
even a fight — and all because he had loitered.

How he tore out of the brambly woods!
How he pounded along the sandy road! But
when he reached the settlement close upon
nightfall, the storekeeper's wife told him that
the men had gone long ago.

" They war powerful special ter git off
early," she added, " 'kase they wanted ter be
thar 'fore Old Daddy drapped off ter sleep.
Some o' them foolish, slack-jawed boys ter the

store ter-day riled the old man's feelin's, an' they 'lowed ter patch up the peace with him, an' let him an' Jonas know ez they never meant no harm."

This suggestion buoyed up the boy's heart to some degree as he toiled along the " short cut " homeward through the heavy shades of the gloomy woods and the mystic effects of the red rising moon. But he was not altogether without anxiety until, as he drew within sight of the log cabin on the slope of the ravine, he heard Old Daddy piping pacifically to the guests about " my son," and Jonas Creyshaw's jolly laughter.

The moon was golden now; Si could see its brilliant shafts of light strike aslant upon the smooth surface of the cliff that formed the opposite side of Old Daddy's Window. He stopped short in the deep shadow of the more rugged crag. The vines and bushes that draped its many jagged ledges dripped with dew. The boughs of an old oak, which grew close by, swayed gently in the breeze. Hidden by its huge bole, Si cast an apprehensive glance toward the house where his elders sat.

Certainly no one was thinking of him now.

" This air my chance fur that young ow*el* — ef ever," he said to himself.

The owl's nest was in the hollow of the tree. The trunk was far too bulky to admit of climbing, and the lowest branches were well out of the boy's reach. Some thirty feet from the ground, however, one of the boughs touched the crag. By clambering up its rugged, irregular ledges, making a zigzag across its whole breadth to the right and then a similar zigzag to the left, Si might gain a position which would enable him to clutch this bough of the tree. Thence he could scramble along to the owl's stronghold.

He hesitated. He knew his elders would disapprove of so reckless an undertaking as climbing about Old Daddy's Window, for in venturing toward its outer verge, a false step, a crumbling ledge, the snapping of a vine, would fling him down the sheer precipice into the depths below.

His hankering for a pet owl had nevertheless brought him here more than once. It
was only yesterday evening — before he had
heard of the ghost's appearance, however —
that he had made his last futile attempt.

He looked up doubtfully. "I ain't ez
strong ez — ez some folks," he admitted.

"But then, come ter think of it," he argued astutely, "I don't weigh nuthin' sca'cely,
an' thar ain't much of me ter hev ter haul up
thar."

He flung off his hat, he laid his wiry hands
upon the wild grape-vines, he felt with his
bare feet for the familiar niches and jagged
edges, and up he went, working steadily to the
right, across the broad face of the cliff.

Its heavy shadow concealed him from view.
Only one ledge, at the extreme verge of the
crag, jutted out into the full moonbeams. But
this, by reason of the intervening bushes and
vines, could not be seen by those who sat in
the cabin porch on the slope of the ravine,
and he was glad to have light just here, for
it was the most perilous point of his enter-

prise. By deft scrambling, however, he suc-
ceeded in getting on the moonlit ledge.

" I clumb like a painter ! " he declared triumphantly.

He rested there for a moment before at-
tempting to reach the vines high up on the
left hand, which he must grasp in order to
draw himself up into the shadowy niche in the
rock, and begin his zigzag course back again
across the face of the cliff to the projecting
bough of the tree.

But suddenly, as he still stood motionless
on the ledge in the full radiance of the moon,
the clamor of frightened voices sounded at
the house. Until now he had forgotten all
about the ghost. He turned, horror-stricken.

There was the frightful thing, plainly defined against the smooth surface of the opposite cliff — some thirty feet distant — that
formed the other side of Old Daddy's Window.

And certainly there are mighty few dan-
cers such as that ghost! It lunged actively
toward the precipice. It suddenly dashed
wildly back — gyrating continually with sin-

gularly nimble feet, flinging wiry arms aloft and maintaining a sinister silence, while the frightened clamor at the house grew ever louder and more shrill.

Several minutes elapsed before Si recognized something peculiarly familiar in the ghost's wiry nimbleness — before he realized that the shadow of the cliff on which he stood reached across the ravine to the base of the opposite cliff, and that the figure which had caused so much alarm was only his own shadow cast upon its perpendicular surface.

He stopped short in those antics which had been induced by mortal terror; of course, his shadow, too, was still instantly. It stood upon the brink of the precipice which seems the sill of Old Daddy's Window, and showed distinctly on the smooth face of the cliff opposite to him.

He understood, after a moment's reflection, how it was that as he had climbed up on the ledge in the full moonlight his shadow had seemed to rise gradually from the vague depths below the insurmountable precipice.

He sprang nimbly upward to seize the vines that shielded him from the observation of the ghost-seers on the cabin porch, and as he caught them and swung himself suddenly from the moonlit ledge into the gloomy shade, he noticed that his shadow seemed to fling its arms wildly above its head, and disappeared upward.

"That air jes' what dad seen las' night when I war down hyar afore, a-figurin' ter ketch that thar leetle ow*el*," he said to himself when he had reached the tree and sat in a crotch, panting and excited.

After a moment, regardless of the coveted owl, he swung down from branch to branch, dropped easily from the lowest upon the ground, picked up his hat, and prepared to skulk along the "short cut," strike the road, and come home by that route as if he had just returned from the settlement.

"'Kase," he argued sagely, "ef them skeered-ter-death grown folks war ter find out ez *I* war the *harnt* — I mean ez the *harnt* war *me* — ennyhow," he concluded desperately, "I'd KETCH it — sure!"

So impressed was he with this idea that he discreetly held his tongue.

And from that day to this, Jonas Creyshaw and his friends have been unable to solve the mystery of Old Daddy's Window.

CHAPTER I

THERE was the grim Big Injun Mountain to the right, with its bare, beetling sandstone crags. There was the long line of cherty hills to the left, covered by a dark growth of stunted pines. Between lay that melancholy stretch of sterility known as Poor Valley, — the poorest of the several valleys in Tennessee thus piteously denominated, because of the sorry contrast which they present to the rich coves and fertile vales so usual among the mountains of the State.

How poor the soil was, Ike Hooden might bitterly testify; for ever since he could hold a plough he had, year after year, followed the old "bull-tongue" through the furrows of the sandy fields which lay around the log cabin at the base of the mountain. In the intervals of "crappin'" he worked at the forge with his stepfather, for close at hand, in the shadow of a great jutting cliff, lurked a dark little shanty of unhewn logs that was a blacksmith's shop.

When he first began this labor, he was, perhaps, the youngest striker that ever wielded a sledge. Now, at eighteen, he had become expert at the trade, and his muscles were admirably developed. He was tall and robust, and he had never an ache nor an ill, except in his aching heart. But his heart was sore, for in the shop he found oaths and harsh treatment, and even at home these pursued him; while outside, desolation was set like a seal on Poor Valley.

One drear autumnal afternoon, when the sky was dull, a dense white mist overspread the valley. As Ike plodded up the steep mountain side, the vapor followed him, creeping silently along the deep ravines and chasms, till at length it overtook and enveloped him. Then only a few feet of the familiar path remained visible.

Suddenly he stopped short and stared. A

dim, distorted something was peering at him
from over the top of a big boulder. It was
moving — it nodded at him. Then he indistinctly recognized it as a tall, conical
hat. There seemed a sort of featureless face
below it.

A thrill of fear crept through him. His
hands grew cold and shook in his pockets.
He leaned forward, gazing intently into the
thick fog.

An odd distortion crossed the vague, featureless face — like a leer, perhaps. Once
more the tall, conical hat nodded fantastically.

" Ef ye do that agin," cried Ike, in sudden
anger, all his pluck coming back with a rush,
" I 'll gin ye a lick ez will weld yer head an'
the boulder together ! "

He lifted his clenched fist and shook it.

" Haw ! haw ! haw ! " laughed the man in
the mist.

Ike cooled off abruptly. He had been
kicked and cuffed half his life, but he had
never been laughed at. Ridicule tamed him.
He was ashamed, and he remembered that he

had been afraid, for he had thought the man was some " roamin' harnt."

" I dunno," said Ike sulkily, " ez ye hev got enny call ter pounce so suddint out'n the fog, an' go ter noddin' that cur'ous way ter folks ez can't half see ye."

" I never knowed afore," said the man in the mist, with mock apology in his tone and in the fantastic gyrations of his nodding hat, " ez it air you-uns ez owns this mounting." He looked derisively at Ike from head to foot. " Ye air the biggest man in Tennessee, ain't ye ? "

" Naw ! " said Ike shortly, feeling painfully awkward, as an overgrown boy is apt to do.

" Waal, from yer height, I mought hev thunk ye war that big Injun that the old folks tells about," and the stranger broke suddenly into a hoarse, quavering chant : —

> " ' A red man lived in Tennessee,
>   Mighty big Injun, sure !
>   He growed ez high ez the tallest tree,
>   An' he sez, sez he, " Big Injun, me ! "
>   Mighty big Injun, sure ! '

"Waal, waal," in a pensive voice, "so ye ain't him? I'm powerful glad ye tole me that, sonny, 'kase I mought hev got skeered hyar in the woods by myself with that big Injun."

He laughed boisterously, and began to sing again : —

> "'Settlers blazed out a road, ye see,
>   Mighty big Injun, sure !
>   He combed thar hair with a knife. Sez he,
> "It's combed fur good ! Big Injun, me !"
>   Mighty big Injun, sure !'"

He broke out laughing afresh, and Ike, abashed and indignant, was about to pass on, when the man gayly balanced himself on one foot, as if he were about to dance a grotesque jig, and held out at arm's length a big silver coin.

It was a dollar. That meant a great deal to Ike, for he earned no money he could call his own.

"Free an' enlightened citizen o' these Nunited States," the man addressed him with mock solemnity, "I brung this dollar hyar fur you-uns."

"What air ye layin' off fur me ter do?" asked Ike.

The man grew abruptly grave. "Jes' stable this hyar critter fur a night an' day."

For the first time Ike became aware of a horse's flank, dimly seen on the other side of the boulder.

"Ter-morrer night ride him up ter my house on the mounting. Ye hev hearn tell o' me, hain't ye, Jedge? My name's Grig Beemy. Don't kem till night, 'kase I won't be thar till then. I hev got ter stop yander — yander" — he looked about uncertainly, "yander ter the sawmill till then, 'kase I promised ter holp work thar some. I'll gin ye the dollar now," he added liberally, as an extra inducement.

"I'll be powerful glad ter do that thar job fur a dollar," said Ike, thinking, with a glow of self-gratulation, of the corn which he had raised in his scanty leisure on his own little patch of ground, and which he might use to feed the animal.

"But hold yer jaw 'bout'n it, boy. Yer

stepdad would n't let the beastis stay thar a minute ef he knowed it, 'kase — waal — 'kase me an' him hev hed words. Slip the beastis in on the sly. Pearce Tallam don't feed an' tend ter his critters nohow. I hev hearn ez his boys do that job, so he ain't like ter find it out. On the sly — that 's the trade."

Ike hesitated.

Once more the man teetered on one foot, and held out the coin temptingly. But Ike's better instincts came to his aid.

" That barn b'longs ter Pearce Tallam. I puts nuthin' thar 'thout his knowin' it. I ain't a fox, nur a mink, nur su'thin wild, ter go skulkin' 'bout on the sly."

Then he pressed hastily on out of temptation's way.

" Haw ! haw ! haw !" laughed the man in the mist.

There was no mirth in the tones now ; his laugh was a bitter gibe. As it followed Ike, it reminded him that the man had not yet moved from beside the boulder, or he would have heard the thud of the horse's hoofs.

He turned and glanced back. The opaque white mist was dense about him, and he could see nothing. As he stood still, he heard a muttered oath, and after a time the man cleared his throat in a rasping fashion, as if the oath had stuck in it.

Ike understood at last. The man was waiting for somebody. And this was strange, here in the thick fog on the bleak mountain-side. But Ike said to himself that it was no concern of his, and plodded steadily on, till he reached a dark little log house, above which towered a flaring yellow hickory tree.

Within, ranged on benches, were homespun-clad mountain children. A high-shouldered, elderly man sat at a table near the deep fire-place, where a huge backlog was smoulder-ing. Through the cobwebbed window-panes the mists looked in.

Ike did not speak as he stood on the thresh-old, but his greedy glance at the scholars' books enlightened the pedagogue. " Do you want to come to school ? " he asked.

Then the boy's long-cherished grievance

burst forth. "They hev tole me ez how it air agin the law, bein' ez I lives out'n the *dee*stric'."

The teacher elevated his grizzled eyebrows, and Ike said, "I kem hyar ter ax ye ef that be a true word. I 'lowed ez mebbe my dad tole me that word jes' ter hender me, an' keep me at the forge. It riles me powerful ter hev ter be an ignorunt all my days."

To a stranger, this reflection on his "dad" seemed unbecoming. The teacher's sympathy ebbed. He looked severely at the boy's pale, anxious face, as he coldly said that he could teach no pupils who resided outside his school district, except out of regular school hours, and with a charge for tuition.

Ike Hooden had no money. He nodded suddenly in farewell, the door closed, and when the schoolmaster, in returning compassion, opened it after him, and peered out into the impenetrable mist, the boy was nowhere to be seen. He had taken his despair by the hand, and together they went down, down into the depths of Poor Valley.

He stood so sorely in need of a little kindness that he felt grateful for the friendly aspect of his stepbrother, whom he met just before he reached the shop.

"'Pears like ye air toler'ble late a-gittin' home, Ike," said Jube. "I done ye the favior ter feed the critters. I 'lowed ez ye would do ez much fur me some day. I'll feed 'em agin in the mornin', ef ye'll forge me three lenks ter my trace-chain ter-night, arter dad hev gone home."

Now this broad-faced, sandy-haired, undersized boy, who was two or three years younger than Ike, and not strong enough for work at the anvil, was a great tactician. It was his habit, in doing a favor, rigorously to exact a set-off, and that night when the blacksmith had left the shop, Jube slouched in.

The flare of the forge-fire illumined with a fitful flicker the dark interior, showing the rod across the corner with its jingling weight of horseshoes, a ploughshare on the ground, the barrel of water, the low window, and casting upon the wall a grotesque shadow of Jube's dodging figure as he began to ply the bellows.

Presently he left off, the panting roar ceased, the hot iron was laid on the anvil, and his dodging image on the wall was replaced by an immense shadow of Ike's big right arm as he raised it. The blows fell fast; the sparks showered about. All the air was ajar with the resonant clamor of the hammer, and the anvil sang and sang, shrill and clear. When the iron was hammered cold, Jube broke the momentary silence.

"I hev got," he droned, as if he were reciting something made familiar by repetition, "two roosters, 'leven hens, an' three pullets."

There was a long pause, and then he chanted, "One o' the roosters air a Dominicky."

He walked over to the anvil and struck it with a small bit of metal which he held concealed in his hand.

"I hev got two shoats, a bag o' dried peaches, two geese, an' I'm tradin' with mam fur a gayn-der."

He quietly slipped the small bit of shining metal in his pocket.

"I hev got," he droned, waxing very impressive, "a red heifer."

Ike paused meditatively, his hammer in his hand. A new hope was dawning within him. He knew what was meant by Jube, who often recited the list of his possessions, seeking to rouse enough envy to induce Ike to exchange for the "lay out" his interest in a certain gray mare.

Now the mare really belonged to Ike, having come to him from his paternal grandfather. This was all of value that the old man had left; for the deserted log hut, rotting on another bleak waste farther down in Poor Valley, was worth only a sigh for the home that it once was, — worth, too, perhaps, the thanks of those it sheltered now, the rat and the owl.

The mare had worked for Pearce Tallam in the plough, under the saddle, and in the wagon all the years since. But one day, when the boy fell into a rage, — for he, too,

had a difficult temper, — and declared that
he would sell her and go forth from Poor
Valley never to return, he was met by the
question, "Hain't the mare lived off'n my
fields, an' hain't I gin ye yer grub, an' clothes,
an' the roof that kivers ye?"

Thus Pearce Tallam had disputed his right
to sell the mare. But it had more than once
occurred to him that the blacksmith would
not object to Jube's buying her.

Hitherto Ike had not coveted Jube's varie-
gated possessions. But now he wanted money
for schooling. It was true he could hardly
turn these into cash, for in this region farm
produce of every description is received at
the country stores in exchange for powder,
salt, and similar necessities, and thus there is
little need for money, and very little is in
circulation.

Still, Ike reflected that he might now and
then get a small sum at the store, or perhaps
the schoolmaster might barter " l'arnin' " for
the heifer or the shoats.

His hesitation was not lost upon Jube, who

offered a culminating inducement to clinch the trade. He suddenly stood erect, teetered fantastically on one foot, as if about to begin to dance, and held out a glittering silver dollar.

The hammer fell from Ike's hands upon the anvil. "'T war ye ez Grig Beemy war a-waitin' fur thar on the mounting in the mist!" he cried out, recognizing the man's odd gesture, which Jube had unconsciously imitated.

Doubtless the dollar was offered to Jube afterward, exactly as it had been offered to him. And Jube had taken it. The imitative monkey thrust it hastily into his pocket, and came down from his fantastic toe, and stood soberly enough on his two feet.

"Grig Beemy gin ye that thar dollar," said Ike.

Jube sullenly denied it. "He never, now!"

"His critter hev got no call ter be in dad's barn."

"His critter ain't hyar," protested Jube. "This dollar war gin me in trade ter the settlemint."

Ike remembered the queer gesture. How could Jube have repeated it if he had not seen it? He broke into a sarcastic laugh.

"That's how kem ye war so powerful 'commodatin' ez ter feed the critters. Ye 'lowed ez I would n't see the strange beastis, an' then tell dad. Foolin' me war a part o' yer trade, I reckon."

Jube made no reply.

"Ef ye war ez big ez me, or bigger, I'd thrash ye out'n yer boots fur this trick. Ye don't want no lenks ter yer chain. Ye jes' want ter be sure o' keepin' me out'n the barn. Waal — thar air yer lenks."

He caught up the tongs and held the links in the fire with one hand while he worked the bellows with the other. Then he laid them red-hot upon the anvil. His rapid blows crushed them to a shapeless mass. "And now — thar they ain't."

Jube did not linger long. He was in terror lest Ike should tell his father. But Ike did not think this was his duty. In fact, neither boy imagined that the affair involved anything more serious than stabling a horse without the knowledge of the owner of the shelter.

When Ike was alone a little later, an unaccustomed sound caused him to glance toward the window.

Something outside was passing it. His position was such that he could not see the object itself, but upon the perpendicular gray wall of the crag close at hand, and distinctly defined in the yellow flare that flickered out through the window from the fire of the forge, the gigantic shadow of a horse's head glided by.

He understood in an instant that Jube had slipped the animal out of the barn, and was hiding him in the misty woods, expecting that Ike would acquaint his father with the facts. He had so managed that these facts would seem lies, if Pearce Tallam should examine the premises and find no horse there.

All the next day the white mist clung shroud-like to Poor Valley. The shadows of evening were sifting through it, when Ike's

mother went to the shop, much perturbed
because the cow had not come, and she could
not find Jube to send after her.

"Ike kin go, I reckon," said the blacksmith.

So Ike mounted his mare and set out
through the thick white vapor. He had divined the cause of Jube's absence, and experienced no surprise when on the summit of
the mountain he overtook him, riding the
strange horse, on his way to Beemy's house.

"I s'pose that critter air yourn, an' ye
mus' hev bought him fur a pound o' dried
peaches, or sech, up thar ter the settle*mint*,"
sneered Ike.

Jube was about to reply, but he glanced
back into the dense mist with a changing
expression.

"Hesh up!" he said softly. "What's
that?"

It was the regular beat of horses' hoofs,
coming at a fair pace along the road on the
summit of the mountain. The riders were
talking excitedly.

"I tell ye, ef I could git a glimpse o' the man ez stole that thar horse, it would go powerful hard with me not to let daylight through him. I brung this hyar shootin'-iron along o' purpose. Waal, waal, though, seein' ez ye air the sheriff, I'll hev ter leave it be ez you-uns say. I would n't know the man from Adam; but ye can't miss the critter, — big chestnut, with a star in his forehead, an'"—

Something strange had happened. At the sound of the voice the horse pricked up his ears, turned short round in the road, and neighed joyfully.

The boys looked at each other with white faces. They understood at last. Jube was mounted on a stolen horse within a hundred yards of the pursuing owner and the officers of the law. Could explanations — words, mere words — clear him in the teeth of this fact?

"Drap out'n the saddle, turn the critter loose in the road, an' take ter the woods," urged Ike.

"They'll sarch an' ketch me," quavered Jube.

He was frantic at the idea of being captured on the horse's back, but if it should come to a race, he preferred trusting to the chestnut's four legs rather than to his own two.

Ike hesitated. Jube had brought the difficulty all on himself, and surely it was not incumbent on Ike to share the danger. But he was swayed by a sudden uncontrollable impulse.

" Drap off'n the critter, turn him loose, an' I'll lope down the road a piece, an' they'll foller me, in the mist."

He might have done a wiser thing. But it was a tough problem at best, and he had only a moment in which to decide.

In that swift, confused second he saw Jube slide from the saddle and disappear in the mist as if he had been caught up in the clouds. He heard the horse's hoofs striking against the stones as he trotted off, whinnying, to meet his master. There was a momentary clamor among the men, and then with whip and spur they pressed on to capture the supposed malefactor.

CHAPTER II

All at once it occurred to Ike, as he galloped down the road, that when they overtook him, they would think that he was the thief, and that he had been leading the horse. He had been so strong in his own innocence that the possibility that they might suspect him had not before entered his mind.

He had intended only to divert the pursuit from Jube, who, although free from any great wrong-doing, was exposed to the most serious misconstruction. The knowledge of the pursuers' revolvers had made this a hard thing to do, but otherwise he had not thought of himself, nor of what he should say when overtaken.

They would question him; he must answer. Would they believe his story? Could he support it? Grig Beemy of course would deny it. And Jube — had he not known how Jube could lie? Would he not fear that the truth might somehow involve him with the horse-thief?

Ike, with despair in his heart, urged his mare to her utmost speed, knowing now the danger he was in as a suspected horse-thief. Suddenly, from among his pursuers, a tiny jet of flame flared out into the dense gray atmosphere, something whizzed through the branches of the trees above his head, and a sharp report jarred the mists.

Perhaps the officer fired into the air, merely to intimidate the supposed criminal and induce him to surrender. But now the boy could not stop. He had lost control of the mare. Frightened beyond measure by the report of the pistol, she was in full run.

On she dashed, down sharp declivities, up steep ascents, and then away and away, with a great burst of speed, along a level sandy stretch.

The black night was falling like a pall upon the white, shrouded day. Ike knew less where he was than the mare did; he was trusting to her instinct to carry him to her stable. More than once the low branches of a tree struck him, almost tearing him from the saddle, but he clung frantically to the mane of the frightened animal, and on and on she swept, with the horsemen thundering behind.

He could hear nothing but their heavy, continuous tramp. He could see nothing, until suddenly a dim, pure light was shining in front of him, on his own level, it seemed. He stared at it with starting eyeballs. It cleft the vapors, — they were falling away on either side, — and they reflected it with an illusive, pearly shimmer.

In another moment he knew that he was nearing the abrupt precipice, for that was the moon, riding like a silver boat upon a sea of mist, with a glittering wake behind it, beyond the sharply serrated summit line of the eastern hills.

He could no longer trust to the mare's instinct. He trusted to appearances instead. He sawed away with all his might on the bit, striving to wheel her around in the road.

She resisted, stumbled, then fell upon her knees among a wild confusion of rotting logs and stones that rolled beneath her, as, snorting and angry, she struggled again to her feet. Once more Ike pulled her to the left.

There was a great displacement of earth, a frantic scramble, and together they went over the cliff.

The descent was not absolutely sheer. At the distance of twelve or fourteen feet below, a great bulging shelf of rock projected. They fell upon this. The boy had instantly loosed his hold of the reins, and slipped away from the prostrate animal. The mare, quieted only for a moment by the shock, sprang to her feet, the stones slipped beneath her, and she went headlong over the precipice into the dreary depths of Poor Valley.

The pursuers heard the heavy thud when she struck the ground far below. They paused at the verge of the crag, and talked in eager, excited tones. They did not see the boy, as he sat cowering close to the cliff on the ledge below.

Ike listened in great trepidation to what they were saying; he experienced infinite surprise when presently one of them mentioned Grig Beemy's name.

TOGETHER THEY WENT OVER THE CLIFF

So they knew who had stolen the horse! It was little consolation to Ike, with his mare lying dead at the foot of the cliff, to reflect that if he had had the courage to face the emergency, and rely upon his innocence, his story would only have confirmed their knowledge of the facts.

Although the master of the horse did not know the thief "from Adam," Beemy had been seen with the animal and recognized by others, who, accompanying the sheriff and the owner, had traced him for two days through many wily doublings in the mountain fastnesses.

They now concluded to press on to Beemy's house. Ike knew they would find him there waiting for Jube and the horse. Beemy had feared that he would be followed, and this was the reason that he had desired to rid himself of the animal for a day and night, until he could make sure and feel more secure.

As the horsemen swept round the curve, Ike remembered how close was the road to the cliff. If he had only given the mare her head,

she would have carried him safely around it.
But there she lay dead, way down in Poor
Valley, and he had lost all he owned in the
world.

Night had come, and in the dense darkness
he did not dare to move. Only a step away
was the edge of the precipice, over which the
mare had slipped, and he could not tell how
dangerous was the bluff he must climb to
regain the summit. He felt he must lie here
till dawn.

He was badly jarred by his fall. Time
dragged by wearily, and his bruises pained
him. He knew at length that all the world
slept, — all but himself and some distant
ravening wolf, whose fierce howl ever and
anon set the mists to shivering in Poor Valley
where he prowled. This blood-curdling sound
and his bitter thoughts were but sorry company.

After a long time he fell asleep. Fortunately, he did not stir. When he regained
consciousness and a sense of danger, he found
still around him that dense white vapor,

through which the pale, drear day was slowly
dawning. Above his head was swinging in the
mist a cluster of fox-grapes, with the rime
upon them, and higher still he saw a quivering
red leaf.

It was the leaf of a starveling tree, growing out of a cleft where there was so little
earth that it seemed to draw its sustenance
from the rock. It was a scraggy, stunted
thing, but it was well for him that it had
struck root there, for its branches brushed the
solid, smooth face of the cliff, which he could
not have surmounted but for them and the
grape-vine that had fallen over from the summit and entangled itself among them.

As he climbed the tree, he felt it quake
over the abysses, which the mists still veiled.
He had a sense of elation and achievement
when he gained the top, and it followed him
home. There it suddenly deserted him.

He found Pearce Tallam in a frenzy of rage
at the discovery, which he had made through
Jube's confession, that a stolen horse had been
stabled on his premises. Despite his tyranny

and his fierce, rude temper, he was an honest man and of fair repute. Although he realized that neither boy knew that the animal had been stolen, he gave Jube a lesson which he remembered for many a long day, and Ike also came in for his share of this muscular tuition.

For in the midst of the criminations and recriminations, the violent blacksmith caught up a horseshoe and flung it across the shop, striking Ike with a force that almost stunned him. He was a man in strength, and it was hard for him not to return the blow; but he only walked out of the shop, declaring that he would stay for no more blows.

"Cl'ar out, then!" called out Pearce Tallam after him. "I don't keer ef ye goes fur good."

He met, at the door of the dwelling, a plaintive reproach from his mother. "'Count o' ye not tellin' on Jube, he mought hev been tuk up fur a horse-thief. I dunno what I'd hev done 'thout him," she added, "'long o' raisin' the young tur-r-keys, an' goslin's, an' deedies, an' sech; he hev been a mighty holp ter me. He air more of a son ter me than my own boy."

She did not mean this, but she had said it once half in jest, half in reproach, and then it became a formula of complaint whenever Ike displeased her.

Now he was sore and sensitive. "Take him fur yer son, then!" he cried. "I'm a-goin' out'n Pore Valley, ef I starves fur it. I shows my face hyar no more."

As he shouldered his gun and strode out, he noted the light of the forge-fire quivering on the mist, but he little thought it was the last fire that Pearce Tallam would ever kindle there.

He glanced back again before the dense vapor shut the house from view. His mother was standing in the door, with her baby in her arms, looking after him with a frightened, beseeching face. But his heart was hardened and he kept on, — kept on, with that deft, even tread of the mountaineer, who seems never to hurry, almost to loiter, but gets over the ground with surprising rapidity.

He left the mists and desolation of Poor Valley far behind, but not that frightened, beseeching face. He thought of it more often when he lay down under the shelter of a great rock to sleep than he did of the howl of the wolf which he had heard the night before, not far from here.

Late the next afternoon he came upon the outskirts of a village. He entered it doubtfully, for it seemed metropolitan to him, unaccustomed as he was to anything more imposing than the cross-roads store. But the first sound he heard reassured him. It was the clear, metallic resonance of an anvil, the clanking of a sledge, and the clinking of a hand-hammer.

Here, at the forge, he found work. It had been said in Poor Valley that he was already as good a blacksmith even as Pearce Tallam. He had great natural aptitude for the work, and considerable experience. But his wages only sufficed to pay for his food and lodging. Still, there was a prospect for more, and he was content.

In his leisure he made friends among those of his own age, who took him about the town and enjoyed his amazement. He examined everything wrought in metal with such eager interest, and was so outspoken about his ambition, that they dubbed him Tubal-cain.

He was struck dumb with amazement when, for the first time in his life, he saw a locomotive gliding along the rails, with a glaring headlight and a cloud of flying sparks. Once, when it was motionless on the track, they talked to the engineer, who explained "the workings of the critter," as Ike called it.

The boy understood so readily that the engineer said, after a time, "You're a likely feller, for such a derned ignoramus! Where have you been hid out, all this time?"

"Way down in Pore Valley," said Ike very humbly.

"He's concluded to be a great inventor," said one of his young friends, with a merry wink.

"He's a mighty artificer in iron," said the wit who had named him Tubal-cain.

The engineer looked gravely at Ike. "Why, boy," he admonished him, "the world has got a hundred years the start of you!"

"I kin ketch up," Ike declared sturdily.

"There's something in grit, I reckon," said the engineer. Then his wonderful locomotive glided away, leaving Ike staring after it in silent ecstasy, and his companions dying with laughter.

He started out to overtake the world at a night-school, where his mental quickness contrasted oddly with his slow, stolid demeanor. He worked hard at the forge all day; but everybody was kind.

Outside of Poor Valley life seemed joyous and hopeful; progress and activity were on every hand; and the time he spent here was the happiest he had ever known, — except for the recollection of that frightened, beseeching face which had looked out after him through the closing mists.

He wished he had turned back for a word. He wished his mother might know he was well and happy. He began to feel that he

could go no further without making his
peace with her. So one day he left his
employer with the promise to return the
following week, "ef the Lord spares me an'
nuthin' happens," as the cautious rural formula has it, and set out for his home.

The mists had lifted from it, but the snow
had fallen deep. Poor Valley lay white and
drear — it seemed to him that he had never
before known how drear — between the grim
mountain with its great black crags, its
chasms, its gaunt, naked trees, and the long
line of flinty hills, whose stunted pines bent
with the weight of the snow.

There was no smoke from the chimney of
the blacksmith's shop. There were no foot-
prints about the door. An atmosphere
charged with calamity seemed to hang over
the dwelling. Somehow he knew that a
dreadful thing had happened even before he
opened the door and saw his mother's mournful white face.

She sprang up at the sight of him with a
wild, sobbing cry that was half grief, half

joy. He had only a glimpse of the interior, — of Jube, looking anxious and unnaturally grave; of the listless children, grouped about the fire; of the big, burly blacksmith, with a strange, deep pallor upon his face, and as he shifted his position — why, how was that?

The boy's mother had thrust him out of the door, and closed it behind her. The jar brought down from the low eaves a few feathery flakes of snow, which fell upon her hair as she stood there with him.

"Don't say nuthin' 'bout'n it," she implored. "He can't abide ter hear it spoke of."

"What ails dad's hand?" he asked, bewildered.

"It's gone!" she sobbed. "He war over ter the sawmill the day ye lef' — somehow 'nuther the saw cotched it — the doctor tuk it off."

"His right hand!" cried Ike, appalled.

The blacksmith would never lift a hammer again. And there the forge stood, silent and smokeless.

What this portended, Ike realized as he sat
with them around the fire. Their sterile
fields in Poor Valley had only served to eke
out their subsistence. This year the corn-
crop had failed, and the wheat was hardly
better. The winter had found them without
special provision, but without special anxiety,
for the anvil had always amply supplied their
simple needs.

Now that this misfortune had befallen
them, who could say what was before them
unless Ike would remain and take his stepfather's place at the forge? Ike knew that
this contingency must have occurred to them
as well as to him. He divined it from the
anxious, furtive glances which they one and
all cast upon him from time to time, — even
Pearce Tallam, whose turn it was now to feel
that greatest anguish of calamity, helplessness.

But must he relinquish his hopes, his
chance of an education, that plucky race for
which he was entered to overtake the world
that had a hundred years the start of him,
and be forever a nameless, futureless clod in
Poor Valley?

His mother had the son she had chosen. And surely he owed no duty to Pearce Tallam. The hand that was gone had been a hard hand to him.

He rose at length. He put on his leather apron. " Waal — I mought ez well g' long ter the shop, I reckon," he remarked calmly. " 'Pears like thar 's time yit fur a toler'ble spot o' work afore dark."

It was a hard-won victory. Even then he experienced a sort of satisfaction in knowing that Pearce Tallam must feel humiliated and of small account to be thus utterly dependent for his bread upon the boy whom he had so persistently maltreated. In his pale face Ike saw something of the bitterness he had endured, of his broken spirit, of his humbled pride.

The look smote upon the boy's heart. There was another inward struggle. Then he said, as if it were a result of deep cogitation, —

" Ye 'll hev ter kem over ter the shop, dad, wunst in a while, ter advise 'bout what 's doin'. 'Pears ter me like mos' folks would 'low ez a boy no older 'n me could n't do reg'lar blacksmithin' 'thout some sperienced body along fur sense an' showin'."

The man visibly plucked up a little. Was he, indeed, so useless? "That 's a fac', Ike," he said gently. "I reckon ye kin make out toler'ble — cornsiderin'. But I 'll be along ter holp."

After this Ike realized that he had been working with something tougher than iron, harder than steel, — his own unsubdued nature. He traced an analogy from the forge; and he saw that those strong forces, the fires of conscience and the coercion of duty, had wrought the stubborn metal of his character to a kindly use.

Gradually the relinquishment of his wild, vague ambition began to seem less bitter to him; for it might be that these were the few things over which he should be faithful, — his own forge-fire and his own fiery heart. And so he labors to fulfill his trust.

The spring never comes to Poor Valley.

The summer is a cloud of dust. The autumn shrouds itself in mist. And the winter is snow. But poverty of soil need not imply poverty of soul. And a noble manhood may nobly exist " 'Way Down in Poor Valley."

" Ef the filly war bridle-wise " —

" The filly *air* bridle-wise."

A sullen pause ensued, and the two brothers looked angrily at each other.

The woods were still; the sunshine was
faint and flickering; the low, guttural notes
of a rain-crow broke suddenly on the silence.

Presently Thad, mechanically examining a
bridle which he held in his hand, began again
in an appealing tone: "'Pears like ter me ez
the filly air toler'ble well bruk ter the saddle,
an' she would holp me powerful ter git thar
quicker ter tell dad 'bout'n that thar word ez
war fotched up the mounting. They 'lowed
ez 't war jes' las' night ez them revenue men
raided a still-house, somewhar down thar in
the valley, an' busted the tubs, an' sp'iled the
coppers, an' arrested all the moonshiners ez
war thar. An' ef they war ter find out

'bout'n this hyar still-house over yander in
the gorge, they'd raid it, too. An' thar be
dad," he continued despairingly, "jes' sodden with whiskey an' ez drunk ez a fraish
b'iled ow*el*, an' he would n't hev the sense
nor the showin' ter make them off'cers
onderstand ez he never hed nothin' ter do
with the moonshiners — 'ceptin' ter go ter
thar still-house, an' git drunk along o' them.
An' I dunno whether the off'cers would set
much store by that sayin' ennyhow, an' I
want ter git dad away from thar afore they
kem."

"I don't believe that thar word ez them
men air a-raidin' round the mountings no
more 'n *that!*" and Ben kicked away a pebble
contemptuously.

Thad was in a quiver of anxiety. While
Ben indulged his doubts, the paternal "B'iled
Ow*el*" might at any moment be arrested on a
charge of aiding and abetting in illicit distilling.

"Ye never b'lieve nothin' till ye see it —
ye sateful dunce!" he exclaimed excitedly.

Thus began a fraternal quarrel which neither forgot for years.

Ben turned scarlet. " Waal, then, jes' leave my filly in the barn whar she be now; ye kin travel on Shank's mare ! "

Thad started off up the steep slope. " Ef ye ain't a-hankerin' fur me ter ride that thar filly, ez air ez bridle-wise ez ye be, jes' let's see ye kem on, an' — hender ! "

" I hopes she'll fling ye, an' ye'll git yer neck bruk," Ben called out after him.

" I wish ennything 'ud happen, jes' so be I mought never lay eyes on ye agin," Thad declared.

As he glanced over his shoulder, he saw that his brother was not following, and when he reached the flimsy little barn, there was nothing to prevent him from carrying out his resolution.

Nevertheless, he hesitated as he stood with the door in his hand. A clay-bank filly came instantly to it, but with a sudden impulse he closed it abruptly, and set out on foot along a narrow, brambly path that wound down the mountain side.

He had descended almost to its base before the threatening appearance of the sky caught his attention. A dense black cloud had climbed up from over the opposite hills, and stretched from their jagged summits to the zenith. There it hung in mid-air, its sombre shadow falling across the valley, and reaching high up the craggy slope, where the boy's home was perched. The whole landscape wore that strange, still, expectant aspect which precedes the bursting of a storm.

Suddenly a vivid white flash quivered through the sky. The hills, suffused with its ghastly light, started up in bold relief against the black clouds; even the faint outlines of distant ranges that had disappeared with the strong sunlight reasserted themselves in a pale, illusive fashion, flickering like the unreal mountains of a dream about the vague horizon. A ball of fire had coursed through the air, striking with dazzling coruscations the top of a towering oak, and he heard, amidst the thunder and its clamorous echo, the sharp crash of riving timber.

All at once he had a sense of falling, a sudden pain shot through him, darkness descended, and he knew no more.

When he gradually regained consciousness, it seemed that a long time had elapsed since he was trudging down the mountain side. He could not imagine where he was now. He put out his hand in the intense darkness that enveloped him, and felt the damp mould beside him, — above — below.

For one horrible instant he recalled a sickening story of a man who was negligently buried alive. He had always believed that this was only a fireside fiction invented in the security of the chimney corner; but was it to have a strange confirmation in his own fate? He was pierced with pity for himself, as he heard the despair in his voice when he sent forth a wild, hoarse cry. What a cavernous echo it had!

Again and again, after his lips were closed, that voice of anguish rang out, and then was silent, then fitfully sounded once more on another key. He strove to rise, but the earth

on his breast resisted.   With a great effort he
finally burst through it ; he felt the clods
tumbling about him ; he sat upright ; he
rose to his full height ; and still all was
merged in the densest darkness, and, when
he stretched up his arms as high as he could
reach, he again felt the damp mould.

The truth had begun vaguely to enter his
mind even before, in shifting his position, he
caught sight of a rift in the deep gloom, some
fifteen feet above his head.   Then he realized
that at the moment of the flash of lightning,
unmindful of his footing, he had strayed aside
from the path, stumbled, fallen, and, as it
chanced, was received into one of those un-
suspected apertures in the ground which are
common in all cavernous countries, being
sometimes the entrance to extensive caves,
and which are here denominated " sink-holes."

These cavities were exceedingly frequent in
the valley, on the boundary of which Thad
lived, and his familiarity with them did away
for the moment with all appreciation of the
perplexity and difficulty of the situation.   He
laughed aloud triumphantly.

Instantly these underground chambers broke forth with wild, elfish voices that mimicked his merriment till it died on his lips. He preferred utter loneliness to the vague sense of companionship given by these weird echoes. Somehow the strangeness of all that had happened to him had stirred his imagination, and he could not rid himself of the idea that there were grimacing creatures here with him, whom he could not see, who would only speak when he spoke, and scoffingly iterate his tones.

He was faint, bruised, and exhausted. He had been badly stunned by his fall; but for the soft, shelving earth through which he had crashed, it might have been still worse. He could scarcely move as he began to investigate his precarious plight. Even if he could climb the perpendicular wall above his head, he could not thence gain the aperture, for, as his eyes became more accustomed to the darkness, he discovered that the shape of the roof was like the interior of a roughly defined dome, about the centre of which was this small opening.

" An' a human can't walk on a ceilin' like a fly," he said discontentedly.

" Can't !" cried an echo close at hand.

" Fly !" suggested a distant mocker.

Thad closed his mouth and sat down.

He had moved very cautiously, for he knew that these sink-holes are often the entrance of extensive caverns, and that there might be a deep abyss on any side. He could do nothing but wait and call out now and then, and hope that somebody might soon take the short cut through the woods, and, hearing his voice, come to his relief.

His courage gave way when he reflected that the river would rise with the heavy rain which he could hear steadily splashing through the sink-hole, and for a time all prudent men would go by the beaten road and the ford. No one would care to take the short cut and save three miles' travel at the risk of swimming his horse, for the river was particularly deep just here and spanned only by a foot-bridge, except, perhaps, some fugitive from justice, or the revenue officers on their hurried, reckless raids. This reminded him of the still-house and of " dad " there yet, imbibing whiskey, and sharing the danger of his chosen cronies, the moonshiners.

Ben, at home, would not have his anxiety roused till midnight, at least, by his brother's failure to return from the complicated feat of decoying the drunkard from the distillery. Thad trembled to think what might happen to himself in the interval. If the volume of water pouring down through the sink-hole should increase to any considerable extent, he would be drowned here like a rat. Was he to have his wish, and see his brother never again ?

And poor Ben ! How his own cruel, wicked parting words would scourge him throughout his life, — even when he should grow old !

Thad's eyes filled with tears of prescient pity for his brother's remorse.

" Ef ennything war ter happen hyar, sure enough, I wish he mought always know ez I don't keer nothin' now 'bout'n that thar sayin' o' his'n," he thought wistfully.

He still heard the persistent rain splashing outside. The hollow, unnatural murmur of a subterranean stream rose drearily. Once he sighed heavily, and all the cavernous voices echoed his grief.

When that terrible flash of lightning came, Ben was still on the slope of the mountain where his brother had left him. The next moment he heard the wild whirl of the gusts as they came surging up the valley. He saw the frantic commotion of the woods on distant spurs as the wind advanced, preceded by swirling columns of dust which carried myriads of leaves, twigs, and even great branches rent from the trees, as evidence of its force.

Ben turned, and ran like a deer up the steep ascent. "It 'll blow that thar barn spang off'n the bluff, I 'm thinkin' — an' the filly — Cobe — Cobe ! " he cried out to her as he neared the shanty.

He stopped short, his eyes distended. The door was open. There was no hair nor hoof of the filly within. He could have no doubt that his brother had actually taken his property for this errand against his will.

" That thar boy air no better 'n a low-down horse-thief ! " he declared bitterly.

The gusts struck the little barn. It careened this way and that, and finally the flimsy structure came down with a crash, one of the boards narrowly missing Ben's head as it fell. He had a hard time getting to the house in the teeth of the wind, but its violence only continued a few minutes, and when he was safe within doors he looked out of the window at the silent mists, beginning to steal about the coves and ravines, and at the rain as it fell in serried columns. Long after dark it still beat with unabated persistence on the roof of the log cabin, and splashed and dripped with a chilly, cheerless sound from the low eaves. Sometimes a drop fell down the wide chimney, and hissed upon the red-hot coals, for Ben had piled on the logs and made a famous fire. He could see that his mother now and then paused to listen in the midst of her preparations for supper. Once as she knelt on the hearth, and deftly inserted a knife between the edges of a baking corn-cake and the hoe, she looked up suddenly at Ben without turning the cake. " I hearn the beastis's huff ! " she said.

Ben listened. The fire roared. The rain went moaning down the valley.

" Ye never hearn nothin'," he rejoined.

Nevertheless, she rose and opened the door. The cold air streamed in. The fire-light showed the mists, pressing close in the porch, shivering, and seeming to jostle and nudge each other as they peered in, curiously, upon the warm home-scene, and the smoking supper, and the hilarious children, as if ask-ing of one another how they would like to be human creatures, instead of a part of inani-mate nature, or at best the elusive spirits of the mountains.

There was nothing to be seen without but the mists.

" Thad tuk the filly, ye say fur true ? " she asked, recurring to the subject when supper was over.

Ben nodded. "I hopes ter conscience she'll break his neck," he declared cruelly.

His mother took instant alarm. She turned and looked at him with a face expressive of the keenest anxiety. "'Pears like to me ez the only reason Thad kin be so late a-gittin' back air jes' 'kase it air a toler'ble aggervatin' job a-fotchin' of dad home," she said, striving to reassure herself.

"That air a true word 'bout'n dad, ennyhow," Ben assented bitterly.

His old grandfather suddenly lifted up his voice.

"This night," said the graybeard from out the chimney corner, — "this night, forty years ago, my brother, Ephraim Grimes, fell dead on this cabin floor, an' no man sence kin mark the cause."

A pause ensued. The rain fell. The pallid, shuddering mists looked in at the window.

"Ye ain't a-thinkin'," cried the woman tremulously, "ez the night air one app'inted fur evil?"

The old man did not answer.

" This night," he croaked, leaning over the glowing fire, and kindling his long-stemmed cob-pipe by dexterously scooping up with its bowl a live coal, — " this night, twenty-six years ago, thar war eleven sheep o' mine — ez war teched in the head, or somehows disabled from good sense — an' they jumped off'n the bluff, one arter the other, an' fell haffen way down the mounting, an' bruk thar fool necks 'mongst the boulders. They war dead. Thar shearin's never kem ter much account nuther. 'T war powerful cur'ous, fust an' last."

The woman made a gesture of indifference. " I ain't a-settin' of store by critters when humans is — is— whar they ain't hearn from."

But Ben was susceptible of a " critter " scare.

" I hope, now," he exclaimed, alarmed, " ez that thar triflin' no-'count Thad Grimes ain't a-goin' ter let my filly lame herself, nor nothin', a-travelin' with her this dark night, ez seems ter be a night fur things ter happen on ennyhow. Oh, shucks ! shucks ! " he continued impatiently, " I jes' feels like thar ain't no use o' my tryin' ter live along."

Three of the children who habitually slept in the shed-room had started off to go to bed. As they opened the connecting door, there suddenly resounded a wild commotion within. They shrieked with fright, and banged the door against a strong force which was beginning to push from the other side.

The old grandfather rose, pale and agitated, his pipe falling from his nerveless clasp.

" This night," he said, with white lips and mechanical utterance, — " this night " —

" Satan is in the shed-room ! " shouted the three small boys, as they held fast to the door with a strength far beyond their age and weight. Nevertheless, they were hardly able to cope with the strength on the other side of the door, and it was alternately forced slightly ajar, and then closed with a resounding slam. Once, as the firelight flickered into the dark shed-room, the ignorant, superstitious mountaineers had a fleeting glimpse of an object there which convinced them: they beheld great gleaming, blazing eyes, a burnished hoof, and — yes — a flirting tail.

" I believe it is Satan himself!" cried Ben, with awe in his voice.

In the wild confusion and bewilderment, Ben was somehow vaguely aware that Satan had often been in the shed-room before, — in the antechamber of his own heart. Whenever this heart of his was full of unkindness, and hardened against his brother, although those better fraternal instincts which he kept repressed and dwarfed might repudiate this cruelty under the pretext that he did not really mean it, still the great principle of evil was there in the moral shed-room, clamoring for entrance at the inner doors. And this, we may safely say, may apply to wiser people than poor Ben.

In the midst of the general despair and fright, something suddenly whinnied. At the sound the three small boys fell in a limp, exhausted heap on the floor, and, as the door no longer offered resistance, the unknown visitor pranced in : it was the filly, snorting

and tossing her mane, and once more whinnying shrilly for her supper.

In a moment Ben understood the whole
phenomenon. Thad had left the barn door
unfastened, and, when that terrible flash of
lightning came and the wind arose, the frightened animal had instantly fled to the house
for safety. She had doubtless pushed open
the back door of the shed-room easily enough,
but it had closed behind her, and she had
remained there a supperless prisoner.

The small boys picked themselves up from
among the filly's hoofs, with disconnected ex-
clamations of " Wa-a-a-l, sir ! " while Ben led
the animal out, with a growing impression
that he would try to " live along " for a while,
at all events.

He had led Satan out of the moral shed-
room, as well. The reappearance of the filly
without Thad had raised a great anxiety
about his brother's continued absence. All
at once he began to feel as if those brutal
wishes of his were prophetic, — as if they
were endowed with a malignant power, and

could actually pursue poor Thad to some violent end. He did not understand now how he could have framed the words.

When a fellow really likes his brother, — and most fellows do, — there is scant use or grace or common-sense in keeping up, from mere carelessness, or through an irritable habit, a continual bickering, for these germs of evil are possessed of a marvelous faculty for growth, and some day their gigantic deformities will confront you in deeds of which you once believed yourself incapable.

Ben's hands were trembling as he folded a blanket, and laid it on the animal's back to serve instead of a saddle.

"I'm a-goin' ter the still-house ter see ef Thad ever got thar," he said, when his mother appeared at the door.

He added, "I'm a-gittin' sorter skeered ez su'thin' mought hev happened ter him."

His grandfather hobbled out into the little porch. "Them roads air turrible rough fur that thar filly, ez ain't fairly broke good yit, nor used ter travel," he suggested.

"I'd gin four hunderd fillies, ef I hed 'em, jes' ter know that thar boy air safe an' sound," Ben declared, as he mounted.

He took the short cut, judging that, at the point where it crossed the river, the stream was still fordable. When he heard his brother's piteous cries for help, he quaked to think what might have happened to Thad if he had not recognized the presence of Satan in the moral shed-room, and summarily ejected him. The rainfall had been sufficient to aggregate considerable water in the gullies about the sink-hole, and these, emptying into the cavity and sending a continuous stream over the boy, had served to chill him through and through, and he had a pretty fair chance of being drowned, or dying from cold and exhaustion. Ben pressed on to the still-house at the best speed he could make, and such of the moonshiners as were half sober came out with ropes and a barrel, which they lowered into the cavity. Thad managed to crawl into the barrel, and, after several ineffectual attempts, he was drawn up through the sink-hole.

There was no formal reconciliation between the two boys. It was enough for Ben to feel Thad's reluctance to unloose his eager clutch upon his brother's arms, even after he had been lifted out upon the firm ground. And Thad knew that that complicated sound in Ben's throat was a sob, although, for the sake of the men who stood by, he strove to seem to be coughing.

" Right smart of an idjit, now, ain't ye? " demanded Ben, hustling back, so to speak, the tears that sought to rise in his eyes.

" Waal, stranger, how's yer filly? " retorted Thad, laughing in a gaspy fashion.

There was a tone of forgiveness in the inquiry. The answer caught the same spirit.

" Middlin', — thanky, — jes' middlin'," said Ben.

And then they and " dad " fared home together by the light of the moonshiners' lantern.

BORROWING A HAMMER

On a certain bold crag that juts far over a steep wooded mountain slope a red light was seen one moonless night in June. Sometimes it glowed intensely among the gray mists which hovered above the deep and sombre valley; sometimes it faded. Its life was the breath of the bellows, for a blacksmith's shop stands close beside the road that rambles along the brink of the mountain. Generally after sunset the forge is dark and silent. So when three small boys, approaching the log hut through the gloomy woods, heard the clink! clank! clink! clank! of the hammers, and the metallic echo among the cliffs, they stopped short in astonishment.

"Thar now!" exclaimed Abner Ryder desperately; "dad 's at it fur true!"

"Mebbe he 'll go away arter a while, Ab,"

suggested Jim Gryce, another of the small boys. " Then that 'll gin us our chance."

" Waal, I reckon we kin stiffen up our hearts ter wait," said Ab resignedly.

All three sat down on a log a short distance from the shop, and presently they became so engrossed in their talk that they did not notice when the blacksmith, in the pauses of his work, came to the door for a breath of air. They failed to discreetly lower their voices, and thus they had a listener on whose attention they had not counted.

" Ye see," observed Ab in a high, shrill pipe, " dad sets a heap o' store by his tools. But dad, ye know, air a mighty slack-twisted man. He gits his tools lost " (reprehensively), " he wastes his nails, an' then he 'lows ez how it war *me* ez done it."

He paused impressively in virtuous indignation. A murmur of surprise and sympathy rose from his companions. Then he recommenced.

" Dad air the crankiest man on this hyar mounting ! He won't lend me none o' his

tools nowadays, — not even that thar leetle
hammer o' his'n. An' I 'm obleeged ter hev
that thar leetle hammer an' some nails ter fix a
box fur them young squir'ls what we cotched.
So we 'll jes' hev ter go ter his shop of a night
when he is away, an' — an' — an' borry it ! "

The blacksmith, a tall, powerfully built
man, of an aspect far from jocular, leaned
slightly out of the door, peering in the direction where the three tow-headed urchins
waited. Then he glanced within at a leather
strap, as if he appreciated the appropriateness
of an intimate relation between these objects.
But there was no time for pleasure now. He
was back in his shop in a moment.

His next respite was thus entertained : —

" What makes him work so of a night ? "
asked Jim Gryce.

" Waal," explained Ab in his usual high
key, " he rid ter the settle*mint* this mornin' ;
he hev been a-foolin' round thar all day, an'
the crap air jes' a-sufferin' fur work ! So him
an' Uncle Tobe air layin' thar ploughs in the
shop now, kase they air goin' ter run around

the corn ter-morrer. Workin', though, goes powerful hard with dad enny time. I tole old Bob Peachin that, when I war ter the mill this evenin'. Him an' the t'other men thar laffed mightily at dad. An' I laffed too ! "

There was an angry gleam in Stephen Ryder's stern black eyes as he turned within, seized the tongs, and thrust a piece of iron among the coals, while Tobe, who had been asleep in the window at the back of the shop, rose reluctantly and plied the bellows. The heavy panting broke forth simultaneously with the red flare that quivered out into the dark night. Presently it faded ; the hot iron was whisked upon the anvil, fiery sparks showered about as the rapid blows fell, and the echoing crags kept time with rhythmic beats to the clanking of the sledge and the clinking of the hand-hammer. The stars, high above the far-stretching mountains, seemed to throb in unison, until suddenly the blacksmith dealt a sharp blow on the face of the anvil as a signal to his striker to cease, and the forge was silent.

As he leaned against the jamb of the door, mechanically adjusting his leather apron, he heard Ab's voice again.

"Old Bob say he ain't no 'count sca'cely. He 'lowed ez he had knowed him many a year, an' fund him a sneakin', deceivin' critter."

The blacksmith was erect in a moment, every fibre tense.

"That ain't the wust," Ab gabbled on. "Old Bob say, though 't ain't known ginerally, ez he air gin ter thievin'. Old Bob 'lowed ter them men, hangin' round the mill, ez he air the biggest thief on the mounting!"

The strong man trembled. His blood rushed tumultuously to his head, then seemed to ebb swiftly away. That this should be said of him to the loafers at the mill! These constituted his little world. And he valued his character as only an honest man can. He was amazed at the boldness of the lie. It had been openly spoken in the presence of his son. One might have thought the boy would come directly to him. But there he sat, glibly re-

tailing it to his small comrades!   It seemed
all so strange that Stephen Ryder fancied
there was surely some mistake.   In the next
moment, however, he was convinced that they
had been talking of him, and of no one else.

" I tole old Bob ez how I thought they
ought n't ter be so hard on him, ez he warn't .
thar to speak for hisself."

All three boys giggled weakly, as if this
were witty.

" But old Bob 'lowed ez ennybody mought
know him by his name.   An' then he told me
that old sayin' : —

> 'Stephen, Stephen, so deceivin',
> That old Satan can't believe him !' "

Here Ben Gryce broke in, begging the
others to go home, and come to " borry " the
hammer next night.   Ab agreed to the latter
proposition, but still sat on the log and talked.
" Old Bob say," he remarked cheerfully,
"that when he do git 'em, he shakes 'em —
shakes the life out'n 'em ! "

This was inexplicable.   Stephen Ryder pondered vainly on it for an instant.   But the

oft-reiterated formula, " Old Bob say," caught his ears, and he was absorbed anew in Ab's discourse.

" Old Bob say ez my mother air one of the best women in this world. But she air so gin ter humoring every critter a-nigh her, an' tends ter 'em so much, an' feeds 'em so high an' hearty, ez they jes' gits good fur nothin' in this world. That's how kem she air eat out'n house an' home now. Old Bob say ez how he air the hongriest critter ! Say he jes' despise ter see him comin' round of meal times. Old Bob say ef he hev got enny good lef' in him, my mother will kill it out yit with kindness."

The blacksmith felt, as he turned back into the shop and roused the sleepy-headed striker, that within the hour all the world had changed for him. These coarse taunts were enough to show in what estimation he was held. And he had fancied himself, in countrified phrase, " respected by all," and had been proud of his standing.

So the bellows began to sigh and pant once

more, and kept the red light flaring athwart the darkness. The people down in the valley looked up at it, glowing like a star that had slipped out of the sky and lodged somehow on the mountain, and wondered what Stephen Ryder could be about so late at night. When he left the shop there was no sign of the boys who had ornamented the log earlier in the evening. He walked up the road to his house, and found his wife sitting alone in the rickety little porch.

"Hev that thar boy gone ter bed?" he asked.

"Waal," she slowly drawled, in a soft, placid voice, "he kem hyar 'bout'n haffen hour ago so nigh crazed ter go ter stay all night with Jim an' Benny Gryce ez I hed ter let him. Old man Gryce rid by hyar in his wagon on his way home from the settle*mint.* So Ab went off with the Gryce boys an' thar gran'dad."

Thus the blacksmith concluded his tools were not liable to be "borrowed" that night. He had a scheme to insure their safety for the future, but in order to avoid his wife's remonstrances on Ab's behalf, he told her nothing of it, nor of what he had overheard.

Early the next morning he set out for the mill, intending to confront "old Bob" and demand retraction. The road down the deep, wild ravine was rugged, and he jogged along slowly until at last he came within sight of the crazy, weather-beaten old building tottering precariously on the brink of the impetuous torrent which gashed the mountain side. Crags towered above it; vines and mosses clung to its walls; it was a dank, cool, shady place, but noisy enough with the turmoil of its primitive machinery and the loud, hoarse voices of the loungers striving to make themselves heard above the uproar. There were several of these idle mountaineers aimlessly strolling among the bags of corn and wheat that were piled about. Long, dusty cobwebs hung from the rafters. Sometimes a rat, powdered white with flour and rendered reckless by high living, raced boldly across the floor. The golden grain poured ceaselessly through the hopper, and leaning against it was the miller, a tall, stoop-shouldered man about forty years of age, with a floury smile lurking in his beard and a twinkle in his good-humored eyes overhung by heavy, mealy eyebrows.

" Waal, Steve," yelled the miller, shambling forward as the blacksmith appeared in the doorway. " Come 'long in. Whar 's yer grist ? "

" I hev got no grist ! " thundered Steve, sternly.

" Waal — ye 're jes' ez welcome," said the miller, not noticing the rigid lines of the blacksmith's face, accented here and there by cinders, nor the fierceness of the intent dark eyes.

" I reckon I 'm powerful welcome ! " sneered Stephen Ryder.

The tone attracted " old Bob's " attention. " What ails ye, Steve ? " he asked, surprised.

" I 'm a deceivin', sneakin' critter — hey," shouted the visitor, shaking his big fist; he had intended to be calm, but his long-repressed fury had found vent at last.

The miller drew back hastily, astonishment and fear mingled in a pallid paste, as it were, with the flour on his face.

The six startled on-lookers stood as if petrified.

"Ye say I'm a thief!—a thief!—a thief!"

With the odious word Ryder made a frantic lunge at the miller, who dodged his strong right arm at the moment when his foot struck against a bag of corn lying on the floor and he stumbled. He recovered his equilibrium instantly. But the six bystanders had seized him.

"Hold him hard, folkses!" cried honest Bob Peachin. "Hold hard! I'll tell ye what ails him — though ye must n't let on ter him —he air teched in the head!"

He winked at them with a confidential intention as he roared this out, forgetting in his excitement that mental infirmity does not impair the sense of hearing. This folly on his part was a salutary thing for Stephen Ryder. It calmed him instantly. He felt that he had need for caution. A fearful vista of possibilities opened before him. He remembered having seen in his childhood a man reputed to be suddenly bereft of reason, but who he believed was entirely sane, bound hand and foot, and every word, every groan, every effort to free himself, accounted the demonstration of a maniac. This fate was imminent for him. They were seven to one. He trembled as he felt their hands pressing upon the swelling muscles of his arms. With an abrupt realization of his great strength, he waited for a momentary relaxation of their clutch, then with a mighty wrench he burst loose from them, flung himself upon his mare, and dashed off at full speed.

He did no work that afternoon, although the corn was " suffering." He sat after dinner smoking his pipe on the porch of his log cabin, while he moodily watched the big shadow of the mountain creeping silently over the wooded valley as the sun got on the down grade. Deep glooms began to lurk among the ravines of the great ridge opposite.

The shimmering blue summits in the distance were purpling. A redbird, alert, crested, and with a brilliant eye, perched idly on the vines about the porch, having relinquished for the day the job of teaching a small, stubby imitation of himself to fly. The shocks of wheat in the bare field close by had turned a rich red gold in the lengthening rays before Stephen Ryder realized that night was close at hand.

All at once he heard a discordant noise which he knew that Ab Ryder called " singing," and presently the boy appeared in the distance, his mouth stretched, his tattered hat stuck on the back of his tow-head, his bare feet dusty, his homespun cotton trousers rolled up airily about his knees, his single suspender supporting the structure. His father laughed a little at sight of him, rather sardonically it must be confessed, and saying to his wife that he intended to go to the shop for a while, he rose and strolled off down the road.

When supper was over, however, Ab was

immensely relieved to see that his father had no idea of continuing his work. Consequently the usual routine was to be expected. Generally, when summoned to the evening meal, the blacksmith hastily plunged his head in the barrel of water used to temper steel, thrust off his leather apron, and went up to the house without more ado. He smoked afterward, and lounged about, enjoying the relaxation after his heavy work. He did not go down to lock the shop until bed-time, when he was shutting up the house, the barn, and the corn-crib for the night. In the interval the shop stood deserted and open, and this fact was the basis of Ab's opportunity. To-night there seemed to be no deviation from this custom. He ascertained that his father was smoking his pipe on the porch. Then he went down the road and sat on the log near the shop to wait for the other boys who were to share the risks and profits of borrowing the hammer.

All was still — so still! He fancied that he could hear the tumult of the torrent far away as it dashed over the rocks. A dog suddenly began to bark in the black, black valley — then ceased. He was vaguely over-awed with the " big mountings " for company and the distant stars. He listened eagerly for the first cracking of brush which told him that the other boys were near at hand. Then all three crept along cautiously among the huge boles of the trees, feeling very mysterious and important. When they reached the rude win-dow, Ab sat for a moment on the sill, peering into the intense blackness within.

" It air dark thar, fur true, Ab," said Jim Gryce, growing faint-hearted. " Let 's go back."

" Naw, sir ! Naw, sir !" protested Ab reso-lutely. " I 'm on the borry !"

" How kin we find that thar leetle hammer in sech a dark place ?" urged Jim.

" Waal," explained Ab, in his high key, " dad air mightily welded ter his cranky no-tions. An' he always leaves every tool in the same place edzactly every night. Bound fur me !" he continued in shrill exultation as he slapped his lean leg, " I know whar that thar leetle hammer air sot ter roost ! "

He jumped down from the window inside the shop, and cut a wiry caper.

" I 'm a man o' bone and muscle ! " he bragged. " Kin do ennything."

The other boys followed more quietly. But they had only groped a little distance when Jim Gryce set up a sharp yelp of pain.

" Shet yer mouth — ye pop-eyed cata-mount ! " Ab admonished him. " Dad will hear an' — ah-h-h ! " His own words ended in a shriek. " Oh, my ! " vociferated the " man of bone and muscle," who was certainly, too, a man of extraordinary lung-power. " Oh, my ! The ground is hot — hot ez iron ! They always tole me that Satan would ketch me — an' oh, my ! now he hev done it ! "

He joined the " pop-eyed catamount " in a lively dance with their bare feet on the hot iron bars which were scattered about the ground in every direction. These were heated artistically, so that they might not really scorch the flesh, but would touch the feelings, and

perhaps the conscience. As the third boy's
scream rent the air, and told that he, too,
had encountered a torrid experience, Ab
Ryder became suddenly aware that there
was some one besides themselves in the shop.
He could see nothing; he was only vaguely
conscious of an unexpected presence, and
he fancied that it was in the corner by the
barrel of water.

All at once a gruff voice broke forth.
" I 'm on the borry!" it remarked with fierce
facetiousness. "I want ter borry a boy —
no! a man o' bone an' muscle — fur 'bout a
minit and a quarter!" A strong arm seized
Ab by his collar. He felt himself swept
through the air, soused head foremost into
the barrel of water, then thrust into a corner,
where he was thankful to find there was no
more hot iron.

"I want to borry another boy!" said the
gruff voice. And the "pop-eyed catamount"
was duly ducked.

"'T would pleasure me some ter borry another!" the voice declared with grim humor.

But Ben was the youngest and smallest, and
only led into mischief by the others. They
never knew that the blacksmith relented when
his turn came, and that he got a mere sprin-
kle in comparison with their total immersion.

Then Stephen Ryder set out for home,
followed by a dripping procession. "I'll
l'arn ye ter 'borry' my tools 'thout leave!"
he vociferated as he went along.

When they had reached the house, he faced
round sternly on Ab. "Why n't ye kem an'
tell me ez how the miller say I war a sneakin',
deceivin' critter, an' — an' — an' a thief!"

His wife dropped the dish she was wash-
ing, and it broke unheeded upon the hearth.
Ab stretched his eyes and mouth in amazement.

"Old Bob Peachin never tole me no sech
word sence I been born!" he declared flatly.

"Then what ailed ye ter go an' tell sech
a lie ter Gryce's boys las' night jes' down
thar outside o' the shop?" Stephen Ryder
demanded.

Ab stared at him, evidently bewildered.

"Ye tole 'em," continued the blacksmith, striving to refresh his memory, "ez Bob Peachin say ez how ye mought know I war deceivin' by my bein' named Stephen — an' that I war the hongriest critter — an' "—

" 'T war the t-a-a-a-rrier ! " shouted Ab, " the little rat tarrier ez we war a-talkin' 'bout. He hev been named Steve these six year, old Bob say. He gimme the dog yestiddy, 'kase I 'lowed ez the rats war eatin' us out'n house an' home, an' my mother hed fed up that old cat o' our'n till he won't look at a mice. Old Bob warned me, though, ez Steve, *the tarrier*, air a mighty thief an' deceivin' gin-erally. Old Bob say he reckons my mother will spile the dog with feedin' him, an' kill out what little good he hev got lef' in him with kindness. But I tuk him, an' brung him home ennyhow. An' las' night arter we hed got through talkin' 'bout borryin' (he looked embarrassed) the leetle hammer, we tuk to talkin' 'bout the tarrier. An' yander he is now, asleep on the chil'ren's bed !"

A long pause ensued.

" M'ria," said the blacksmith meekly to his wife, " hev ye tuk notice how the gyarden truck air a-thrivin' ? 'Pears like ter me ez the peas air a-fullin' up consider'ble."

And so the subject changed.

He had it on his conscience, however, to explain the matter to the miller. For the second time old Bob Peachin, and the men at the mill, " laffed mightily at dad." And when Ab had recovered sufficiently from the exhaustion attendant upon borrowing a hammer, he " laffed too."

THE CONSCRIPTS' HOLLOW

CHAPTER I

"I 'm a-goin' ter climb down ter that thar ledge, an' slip round ter the hollow whar them conscripts built thar fire in the old war times."

Nicholas Gregory paused on the verge of the great cliff and cast a sidelong glance at Barney Pratt, who was beating about among the red sumach bushes in the woods close at hand, and now and then stooping to search the heaps of pine needles and dead leaves where they had been blown together on the ground.

"Conscripts!" Barney ejaculated, with a chuckle. "That 's precisely what them men war determinated *not* ter be! They war a-hidin' in the mountings ter git shet o' the conscription."

"Waal, I don't keer ef *ye* names 'em

'conscripts' or no," Nicholas retorted loftily.
"That's what other folks calls 'em. I'm
goin' down ter the hollow, whar they built
thar fire, ter see ef that old missin' tur-r-key-
hen o' our'n hain't hid her nest off 'mongst
them dead chunks, an' sech."

"A tur-r-key ain't sech a powerful fool ez
that," said Barney, coming to the edge of the
precipice and looking over at the ledge, which
ran along the face of the cliff twenty feet
below. "How'd she make out ter fotch
the little tur-r-keys up hyar, when they war
hatched? They'd fall off'n the bluff."

"A tur-r-key what hev stole her nest away
from the folks air fool enough fur ennything," Nicholas declared.

Perhaps he did not really expect to find the
missing fowl in such an out-of-the-way place
as this, but being an adventurous fellow, the
sight of the crag was a temptation. He had
often before clambered down to the ledge,
which led to a great niche in the solid rock,
where one night during the war some men
who were hiding from the conscription had

kindled their fire and cooked their scanty
food. The charred remnants of logs were
still here, but no one ever thought about them
now, except the two boys, who regarded them
as a sort of curiosity.

Sometimes they came and stared at them,
and speculated about them, and declared to
each other that *they* would not consider it a
hardship to go a-soldiering.

Then Nick would tell Barney of a wonderful day when he had driven to the county
town in his uncle's wagon. There was a
parade of militia there, and how grand the
drum had sounded! And as he told it he
would shoulder a smoke-blackened stick, and
stride about in the Conscripts' Hollow, and
feel very brave.

He had no idea in those days how close at
hand was the time when his own courage
should be tried.

"Kem on, Barney!" he urged. "Let's
go down an' sarch fur the tur-r-key."

But Barney had thrown himself down upon
the crag with a long-drawn sigh of fatigue.

"Waal," he replied, in a drowsy tone, "I dunno 'bout'n that. I'm sorter banged out, 'kase I hev had a powerful hard day's work a-bilin' sorghum at our house. I b'lieves I'll rest my bones hyar, an' wait fur ye."

As he spoke, he rolled up one of the coats which they had both thrown off, during their search for the nest on the summit of the cliff, and slipped it under his head. He was far the brighter boy of the two, but his sharp wits seemed to thrive at the expense of his body. He was small and puny, and he was easily fatigued in comparison with big burly Nick, who rarely knew such a sensation, and prided himself upon his toughness.

"Waal, Barney, surely ye air the porest little shoat on G'liath Mounting!" he exclaimed scornfully, as he had often done before. But he made no further attempt to persuade Barney, and began the descent alone.

It was not so difficult a matter for a sure-footed mountaineer like Nick to make his way down to the ledge as one might imagine, for in a certain place the face of the cliff presented a series of jagged edges and projections which afforded him foothold. As he went along, too, he kept a strong grasp upon overhanging vines and bushes that grew out from earth-filled crevices.

He had gone down only a short distance when he paused thoughtfully. "This hyar wind air blowin' powerful brief," he said. "I mought get chilled an' lose my footin'."

He hardly liked to give up the expedition, but he was afraid to continue on his way in the teeth of the mountain wind, cold and strong in the October afternoon. If only he had his heavy jeans coat with him!

"Barney!" he called out, intending to ask his friend to throw it over to him.

There was no answer.

"That thar Barney hev drapped off ter sleep a'ready!" he exclaimed indignantly.

He chanced to glance upward as he was about to call again. There he saw a coat lying on the edge of the cliff, the dangling sleeve fluttering just within his reach. When he dragged it down and discovered that it was

Barney's instead of his own, he was slightly vexed, but it certainly did not seem a matter of great importance.

"That boy hev got *my* coat, an' this is his'n. But law! I'd ruther squeeze myself small enough ter git inter his'n, than ter hev ter yell like a catamount fur an hour an' better ter wake him up, an' make him gimme mine."

He seated himself on a narrow projection of the crag, and began to cautiously put on his friend's coat. He had need to be careful, for a precarious perch like this, with an unmeasured abyss beneath, the far blue sky above, the almost inaccessible face of a cliff on one side, and on the other a distant stretch of mountains, is not exactly the kind of place in which one would prefer to make a toilet. Besides the dangers of his position, he was anxious to do no damage to the coat, which although loose and baggy on Barney, was rather a close fit for Nick.

"I ain't used ter climbin' with a coat on, nohow, an' I mus' be mighty keerful not ter bust Barney's, 'kase it air all the one he hev got," he said to himself as he clambered nimbly down to the ledge.

Then he walked deftly along the narrow shelf, and as he turned abruptly into the immense niche in the cliff called the Conscripts' Hollow, he started back in sudden bewilderment. His heart gave a bound, and then it seemed to stand still.

He hardly recognized the familiar place. There, to be sure, were the walls and the dome-like roof, but upon the dusty sandstone floor were scattered quantities of household articles, such as pots and pails and pans and kettles. There was a great array of brogans, too, and piles of blankets, and bolts of coarse unbleached cotton and jeans cloth.

" Waal, sir ! " he exclaimed, as he gazed at them with wild, uncomprehending eyes.

Then the truth flashed upon him. A story had reached Goliath Mountain some weeks before, to the effect that a cross-roads store, some miles down the valley, had been robbed. The thieves had escaped with the stolen goods, leaving no clue by which they might be identified and brought to justice.

Nick saw that he had made a discovery. Here it was that the robbers had contrived to conceal their plunder, doubtless intending to wait until suspicion lulled, when they could carry it to some distant place, where it could safely be sold.

Suddenly a thought struck him that sent a shiver through every fibre of his body. This store was robbed in a singular manner. No bolt was broken, — no door burst open. There was a window, however, that lacked one pane of glass. The aperture would not admit a man's body. It was believed that the burglars had passed a boy through it, who had handed out the stolen goods.

And now, Nick foolishly argued, if any one should discover that *he* knew where the plunder was hidden, they would believe that *he* was that boy who had robbed the store!

He began to resolve that he would say nothing about what he had seen, — not even to Barney. He thought his safety lay in his silence. Still, he did not want his silence to be to the advantage of wicked men, so he tried to persuade himself that the burglars would soon be traced and captured without the information which he knew it was his duty to give. "Ter be sartain, the officers will kem on this place arter a while," he said meditatively.

Then he shook his head doubtfully. The crag was far from any house, and except the dwellers on Goliath Mountain, few people knew of this great niche in it. "They war sly foxes what stowed away thar plunder hyar!" he exclaimed in despair.

Often, when Nick had before stood in the Conscripts' Hollow, he had imagined that he would make a good soldier. But his idea of a soldier was a fine uniform, and the ra-ta-ta of martial music. He had no conception of that high sense of duty which nerves a man to face danger; even now he did not know that he was a coward as he faltered and feared in the cause of right to encounter suspicion.

Courage! — Nick thought that meant to

crack away at a bear, if you were lucky enough to have the chance; or to kill a rattlesnake, if you had a big heavy stone close at hand; or to scramble about among crags and precipices, if you felt certain of the steadiness of your head and the strength of your muscles. But he did not realize that " courage " could mean the nerve to speak one little word for duty's sake.

He would not speak the word, — he had determined on that, — for might they not think that *he* was the boy who had robbed the store?

He was quivering with excitement when he turned and began to walk along the ledge toward those roughly hewn natural steps by which he had descended. He knew that his agitation rendered his footing insecure. He was afraid of falling into the depths beneath, and he pressed close against the cliff.

On the narrow ledge, hardly two yards distant from the Conscripts' Hollow, a clump of blackberry bushes was growing from a crevice in the rock. They had never before given him trouble; but now, as he brushed hastily past, they seemed to clutch at him with their thorny branches.

As he tore away from them roughly, he did not observe that he had left a fragment of his brown jeans clothing hanging upon the thorns, as a witness to his presence here close to the Conscripts' Hollow, where the stolen goods lay hidden. There was a coarse, dark-colored horn button attached to the bit of brown jeans, which was a three-cornered scrap of his coat. No! of *Barney's* coat. And was it to be a witness against poor Barney, who had not gone near the Conscripts' Hollow, but was lying asleep on the summit of the crag, supposing he had his own coat under his own head?

He did not discover his mistake until some time afterward, for when Nick had slowly and laboriously climbed up the steep face of the cliff, he stripped off his friend's torn coat before he roused him. Barney was awakened by having his pillow dragged rudely from under his head, and when at last he reluctantly opened his eyes on the hazy yellow sunlight, and saw Nick standing near on the great gray crag, he had no idea that this moment was an important crisis in his life.

The wind was coming up the gorge fresh and free; the autumnal foliage, swaying in it, was like the flaunting splendors of red and gold banners; the western ranges had changed from blue to purple, for the sun was sinking.

"It's gittin' toler'ble late, Barney," said Nick. "Let's go." He had on his own coat now, and he was impatient to be off.

"Did ye find the tur-r-key's nest in the Conscripts' Hollow?" asked Barney, with a lazy yawn, and still flat on his back.

"No," said Nick curtly.

Then it occurred to him that it would be safer if his friend should think he had not been in the Hollow. "No," he reiterated, after a pause, "I did n't go down ter the ledge arter all."

He had begun to lie, — where would it end?

"Why n't you-uns go?" demanded Barney, surprised.

" The wind war blowin' so powerful brief,"
Nick replied without a qualm. " So I jes'
s'arched fur a while in the woods back thar
a piece."

In a moment more, Barney rose to his feet,
picked up his coat, and put it on. He did
not notice the torn place, for the garment
was old and worn, and had many ragged
edges. It lacked, however, but one button,
and that missing button was attached to the
triangular bit of brown jeans that fluttered
on the thorny bush close to the Conscripts'
Hollow.

All unconscious of his loss, he went away
in the rich autumnal sunset, leaving it there
as a witness against him.

CHAPTER II

After this, Nicholas Gregory was very steady
at his work for a while. He kept out of the
woods as much as possible, and felt that he
knew more already than was good for him.
Above all, he avoided that big sandstone cliff

and the Conscripts' Hollow, where the goods lay hidden.

He heard no more of the search that had been made for the burglars and their booty, and he congratulated himself on his caution in keeping silent about what he had found.

"Now, ef it hed been that thar wide-mouthed Barney, stid o' me, he'd hev blabbed fust thing, an' they'd all hev thunk ez he war the boy what them scoundrels put through the winder ter steal the folkses' truck. They'd hev jailed him, I reckon."

He had begun to forget his own part in the wrong-doing, — that his silence was helping to screen "them scoundrels" from the law.

This state of mind continued for a week, perhaps. Then he fell to speculating about the stolen goods. He wondered whether they were all there yet, or whether the burglars had managed to carry them away. His curiosity grew so great that several times he was almost at the point of going to see for himself; but one morning, early, when an opportunity to do so was suddenly presented, his courage failed him.

His mother had just come into the log cabin from the hen-house with a woe-begone face.

" I do declar' ! " she exclaimed solemnly, " that I 'm surely the afflictedest 'oman on G'liath Mounting ! An' them young fall tur-r-keys air so spindlin' an' delikit they 'll be the death o' me yit ! "

They were so spindling and delicate that they were the death of themselves. She had just buried three, and her heart and her larder were alike an aching void.

" Three died ter-day, an' two las' Wednesday ! " As she counted them on her fingers she honored each with a shake of the head, so mournful that it might be accounted an obituary in dumb show. " I hev had no sort'n luck with this tur-r-key's brood, an' the t'other hev stole her nest away, an' I hev got sech a mean no-'count set o' chillen they can't find her. Waal ! waal ! waal ! this comin' winter the Lord 'll be *obleeged* ter pervide."

This was washing-day, and as she began to scrub away on the noisy washboard, a sudden thought struck her. " Ye told me two weeks ago an' better, Nick, that ye hed laid off ter sarch the Conscripts' Hollow ; ye 'lowed ye hed been everywhar else. Did ye go thar fur the tur-r-key ? "

She faced him with her dripping arms akimbo.

Nick's face turned red as he answered, " That thar tur-r-key ain't a-nigh thar."

" What ails ye, Nick ? thar 's su'thin' wrong. I kin tell it by yer looks. Ye never hed the grit ter sarch thar, I 'll be bound; did ye, now ? "

Nick could not bring himself to admit having been near the place.

" No," he faltered, " I never sarched thar."

" Ye 'll do it now, though ! " his mother declared triumphantly. " I 'm afeard ter send Jacob on sech a yerrand down the bluffs, kase he air so little he mought fall ; but he air big enough ter go 'long an' watch ye go down ter the Hollow — else ye 'll kem back an' say ye hev sarched thar, when ye ain't been a-nigh the bluff."

There seemed for a moment no escape for Nick. His mother was looking resolutely at him, and Jacob had gotten up briskly from his seat in the chimney-corner. He was a small tow-headed boy with big owlish eyes, and Nick knew from experience that they were very likely to see anything he did *not* do. He must go; and then if at any time the stolen goods should be discovered, Jacob and his mother, and who could say how many besides, would know that he had been to the Conscripts' Hollow, and must have seen what was hidden there.

In that case his silence on the subject would be very suspicious. It would seem as if he had some connection with the burglars, and for that reason tried to conceal the plunder.

He was saying to himself that he would not go — and he must! How could he avoid it? As he glanced uneasily around the room, his eyes chanced to fall on a little object lying on the edge of the shelf just above the washtub.

He made the most of the opportunity. As he slung his hat upon his head with an impatient gesture, he managed to brush the shelf with it and knock the small object into the foaming suds below.

His mother sank into a chair with uplifted hands and eyes.

"The las' cake o' hop yeast!" she cried. "An' how air the bread ter be raised?"

To witness her despair, one would think only jack-screws could do it.

"Surely I *am* the afflictedest 'oman on G'liath Mounting! An' ter-morrer Brother Pete's wife an' his gals air a-comin', and I hed laid off ter hev raised bread."

For "raised bread" is a great rarity and luxury in these parts, the nimble "dodgers" being the staff of life.

"I never went ter do it," muttered Nick.

"Waal, ye kin jes' kerry yer bones down the mounting ter Sister Mirandy's house, an' ax her ter fotch me a cake o' her yeast when she kems up hyar ter-day ter holp me sizin' yarn. Arter that I don't keer what ye does with yerself. Ef ye stays hyar along o' we-uns, ye 'll haul the roof down nex', I reckon. 'Pears like ter me ez boys an' men-folks air powerful awk'ard, useless critters ter keep in a house; they oughter hev pens outside, I 'm a-thinkin'."

She had forgotten about the turkey, and Nick was glad enough to escape on these terms.

It was not until after he had finished his errand at Aunt Mirandy's house that he chanced to think again of the Conscripts' Hollow. As he was slowly lounging back up the mountain, he paused occasionally on the steep slope and looked up at the crags high on the summit, which he could see, now and then, diagonally across a deep cove.

When he came in sight of the one which he had such good reason to remember, he stopped and stood gazing fixedly at it for a long time, wondering again whether the robbers had yet carried off their plunder from its hiding-place.

He was not too distant to distinguish the

Conscripts' Hollow, but from his standpoint, he could not at first determine where was the ledge. He thought he recognized it presently in a black line that seemed drawn across the massive cliff.

But what was that upon it? A moving figure! He gazed at it spell-bound for a moment, as it slowly made its way along toward the Hollow. Then he wanted to see no more; he wanted to know no more. He turned and fled at full speed along the narrow cow-path among the bushes.

Suddenly there was a rustle among them. Something had sprung out into the path with a light bound, and as he ran, he heard a swift step behind him. It seemed a pursuing step, for, as he quickened his pace, it came faster too. It was a longer stride than his; it was gaining upon him. A hand with a grip like a vise fell upon his shoulder, and as he was whirled around and brought face to face with his pursuer, he glanced up and recognized the constable of the district.

This was a tall, muscular man, dressed in

brown jeans, and with a bushy red beard. He knew Nick well, for he, too, was a mountaineer.

" Ye war a-dustin' along toler'ble fast, Nicholas Gregory," he exclaimed; " but nothin' on G'liath Mounting kin beat me a-runnin' 'thout it air a deer. Ye 'll kem along with me now, and stir yer stumps powerful lively, too, kase I hain't got no time ter lose."

" What am I tuk up fur ? " gasped Nick.

" S'picious conduc'," replied the man curtly.

Nick knew no more now than he did before. The officer's next words made matters plainer. " Things look mightily like ye war set hyar ter watch that thar ledge. Ez soon ez ye seen our men a-goin' ter the Conscripts' Hollow ter sarch fur that thar stole truck, ye war a-goin' ter scuttle off an' gin the alarm ter them rascally no-'count burglars. I saw ye and yer looks, and I suspicioned some sech game. Ye don't cheat the law in *this* deestrick — not often ! Ye air the very boy, I reckon, what holped ter rob Blenkins's store.

Whar's the other burglars? Ye'd better tell!"

" I dunno!" cried Nick tremulously. " I never had nothin' ter do with 'em."

" Ye hev told on yerself," the man retorted. " Why did ye stand a-gapin' at the Conscripts' Hollow, ef ye did n't know thar was suthin special thar?"

Nick, in his confusion, could invent no reply, and he was afraid to tell the truth. He looked mutely at the officer, who held his arm and looked down sternly at him.

" Ye air a bad egg, — that's plain. I'll take ye along whether I ketches the other burglars or no."

They toiled up the steep ascent in silence, and before very long were on the summit of the mountain, and within view of the crag.

There on the great gray cliff, in the midst of the lonely woods, were several men whom Nick had never before seen. Their busy figures were darkly defined against the hazy azure of the distant ranges, and as they moved about, their shadows on the ground seemed very busy too, and blotted continually the golden sunshine that everywhere penetrated the thinning masses of red and bronze autumn foliage.

A wagon, close at hand, was already half full of the stolen goods, and a number of men were going cautiously up and down the face of the cliff, bringing articles, or passing them from one to another.

"Well, this *is* a tedious job!" exclaimed the sheriff, John Stebbins by name. He was a quick-witted, good-natured man, but being active in temperament, he was exceedingly impatient of delay. "How long did it take 'em to get all those heavy things down into the Conscripts' Hollow, — hey, bub?" he added, appealing to Nick, who had been brought to his notice by the constable. It was terrible to Nick that they should all speak to him as if he were one of the criminals. He broke out with wild protestations of his innocence, denying, too, that he had had any knowledge of what was hidden in the Conscripts' Hollow.

"Then what made ye run, yander on the slope, when ye seen thar war somebody on the ledge?" demanded the constable.

Nick had a sudden inspiration. "Waal," he faltered, with an explanatory sob, which was at once ludicrous and pathetic, "I war too fur off ter make out fur sure what 't war on the ledge. 'T war black-lookin', an' I 'lowed 't war a b'ar."

All the men laughed at this.

"I sot out ter run ter Aunt Mirandy's house ter borry Job's gun ter kem up hyar, an' mebbe git a crack at him," continued Nick.

"That does n't seem unnatural," said the sheriff. Then he turned to the constable. "This ain't enough to justify us in holding on to the boy, Jim, unless we can fix that scrap with the button on him. Where is it?"

"D' ye know whose coat this kem off'n?" asked the constable, producing a bit of brown jeans, with a dark-colored horn button attached to it. "How 'd it happen ter be stickin' ter them blackberry-bushes on the ledge?"

Nick recognized it in an instant. It was Barney Pratt's button, and a bit of Barney Pratt's coat. But he knew well enough that he himself must have torn it when he wore it down to the Conscripts' Hollow.

He realized that he should have at once told the whole truth of what he knew about the stolen goods. He was well aware that he ought not to suffer the suspicion which had unjustly fallen upon him to be unjustly transferred to Barney, who he knew was innocent.

But he was terribly frightened, and foolishly cautious, and he did not care for justice, nor truth, nor friendship, now. His only anxiety was to save himself.

" That thar piece o' brown jeans an' that button kem off'n Barney Pratt's coat. I'd know 'em anywhar," he answered, more firmly than before. He noted the fact that the searching eyes of both officers were fixed upon his own coat, which was good and whole, and lacked no buttons. He had not even a twinge of conscience just now. In his meanness and cowardice his heart exulted, as he saw that suspicion was gradually lifting its dark shadow from him. He cared not where it might fall next.

"We'll have to let you slide, I reckon," said the sheriff. "But what size is this Barney Pratt?"

"He air a lean, stringy little chap," said Nick.

"Is that so?" said the sheriff. "Well, this is a bit of his coat and his button; and they were found on the ledge, close to the Conscripts' Hollow where the plunder was hid; and he's a small fellow, that maybe could slip through a window-pane. That makes a pretty strong showing against him. We'll go for Barney Pratt!"

CHAPTER III

Barney Pratt expected this day to be a holiday. Very early in the morning his father and mother had jolted off in the wagon to attend the wedding of a cousin, who lived ten miles distant on a neighboring mountain, and they had left him no harder task than to keep the children far enough from the fire, and his paralytic grandmother close enough to it.

This old woman was of benevolent intentions, although she had a stick with which she usually made her wants known by pointing, and in her convulsive clutch the stick often whirled around and around like the sails of a windmill, so that if Barney chanced to come within the circle it described, he got as hard knocks from her feeble arm as he could have had in a tussle with big Nick Gregory.

He was used to dodging it, and so were the smaller children. Without any fear of it they were all sitting on the hearth at the old woman's feet, — Ben and Melissa popping corn in the ashes, and Tom and Andy watching Barney's deft fingers as he made a cornstalk fiddle for them.

Suddenly Barney glanced up and saw his grandmother's stick whirling over his head. Her eyes were fastened eagerly upon the

window, and her lips trembled as she strove
to speak.

"What d' ye want, granny?" he asked.

Then at last it came out, quick and sharp,
and in a convulsive gasp, — "Who air all
that gang o' folks a-comin' yander down the
road?"

Barney jumped up, threw down the fiddle,
and ran to the door with the children at his
heels.   There was a quiver of curiosity among
them, for it was a strange thing that a "gang
o' folks" should be coming down this lonely
mountain road.

They went outside of the log cabin and
stood among the red sumach bushes that
clustered about the door, while the old woman
tottered after them to the threshold, and
peered at the crowd from under her shaking
hand as she shaded her eyes from the sunlight.

Presently a wagon came up with eight or
ten men walking behind it, or riding in it in
the midst of a quantity of miscellaneous
articles of which Barney took no particular

notice. As he went forward, smiling in a frank, fearless way, he recognized a familiar face among the crowd. It was Nick Gregory's, and Barney's smile broadened into a grin of pleasure and welcome.

Then it was that Nick's conscience began to wake up, and to lay hold upon him.

As the sheriff looked at Barney he hesitated. He balanced himself heavily on the wheel, instead of leaping quickly down as he might have done easily enough, for he was a spare man and light on his feet. Nick overheard him speak in a low voice to the constable, who stood just below.

" *That* ain't the fellow, is it, Jim ? "

" That's him, percisely," responded Jim Dow.

" He don't *look* like it," said Stebbins, jumping down at last, but still speaking under his breath.

" Waal, thar ain't no countin' on boys by the *outside* on 'em," returned the constable emphatically ; he had an unruly son of his own.

The sheriff walked up to Barney.

"You're Barney Pratt, are you? Well, youngster, you'll come along with us."

There was silence for a moment. Barney stared at him in amaze. Not until he had caught sight of the constable, whom he knew in his official character, did he understand the full meaning of what had been said. He was under arrest!

As he realized it, everything began to whirl before him. The yellow sunshine, the gorgeously tinted woods, the blue sky, and the silvery mists hovering about the distant mountains, were all confusedly mingled in his failing vision.

He looked as if he were about to faint. But in a few minutes he had partially recovered himself.

"I dunno what this air done ter me fur," he said tremulously, glancing up at the officer whose hand was on his shoulder.

"Hain't ye been doin' nothin' mean lately?" demanded Jim Dow sternly.

Barney shook his head.

"Let's see ef this won't remind ye," said the constable, producing the bit of jeans and the button.

As Nick watched Barney turning the piece of cloth in his hand and examining the button, he felt a terrible pang of remorse. But he was none the less resolved to keep the freedom from danger which he had secured at the expense of his friend. To explain would be merely to exchange places with Barney, and he was silent.

"This hyar looks like a scrap o' my coat," said Barney, utterly unaware of the significance of his words. As he fitted it into the jagged edges of the garment, the officers watched the proceeding closely. "'Pears like ter me ez it war jerked right out thar — yes — kase hyar air the missin' button, too."

His air of unconsciousness puzzled the sheriff. "Do you know where you lost this scrap?" he asked.

"Somewhars 'mongst the briers in the woods, I reckon," replied Barney.

"No; you tore it on a blackberry bush on

the ledge of a bluff ; it was close to the Conscripts' Hollow, where some burglars have
hidden stolen plunder.   I found the scrap and
the button there myself."

Barney felt as if he were dreaming.   How
should his coat be torn on that ledge, where
he had not been since the cloth was woven !

The next words almost stunned him.

"Ye see, sonny," said the constable, "we
believes ye're the boy what holped to rob
Blenkins's store by gittin' through a winder-
pane an' handin' out the stole truck ter the
t'other burglars.   Ye hev holped about that
thar plunder somehows, — else this hyar thing
air a liar !" and he shook the bit of cloth
significantly.

"We'd better set out, Jim," said Stebbins,
turning toward the wagon.   "We'll pass
Blenkins's on the way, and we'll stop and
see if this chap can slip through the window-
pane.   If he can't, it's a point in his favor,
and if he can, it's a point against him.   As
we go, we can try to get him to tell who the
other burglars are."

" Kem on, bubby; we can't stand hyar no longer, a-wastin' the time an' a-burnin' of daylight," said the constable.

Barney seemed to have lost control of his rigid limbs, and he was half-dragged, half-lifted into the wagon by the two officers. The crowd began to fall back and disperse, and he could see the group of " home-folks " at the door. But he gave only one glance at the little log cabin, and then turned his head away. It was a poor home, but if it had been a palace, the pang he felt as he was torn from it could not have been sharper.

In that instant he saw granny as she stood in the doorway, her head shaking nervously and her stick whirling in her uncertain grasp. He knew that she was struggling to say something for his comfort, and he had a terrible moment of fear lest the wagon should begin to move and her feeble voice be lost in the clatter of the wheels. But presently her shrill tones rang out, " No harm kin kem, sonny, ter them ez hev done no harm. All that happens works tergether fur good, an' the will o' God."

Little breath as she had left, it had done good service to-day, — it had brought a drop of balm to the poor boy's heart. He did not look at her again, but he knew that she was still standing in the doorway among the clustering red leaves, whirling her stick, and shaking with the palsy, but determined to see the last of him.

And now the wagon was rolling off, and a piteous wail went up from the children, who understood nothing except that Barney was being carried away against his will. Little four-year-old Melissa — she always seemed a beauty to Barney, with her yellow hair, and her blue-checked cotton dress, and her dimpled white bare feet — ran after the wagon until the tears blinded her, and she fell in the road, and lay there in the dust, sobbing.

Then Barney found his voice. His father and mother would not return until to-morrow, and the thought of what might happen at home, with nobody there but the helpless old grandmother and the little children, made him forget his own troubles for the time.

"Take good keer o' the t'other chillen, Andy!" he shouted out to the next oldest boy, thus making him a deputy-guardian of the family, "an' pick Melissy up out'n the dust, an' be sure ye keeps granny's cheer close enough ter the fire!"

Then he turned back again. He could still hear Melissa sobbing. He wondered why the two men in the wagon looked persistently in the opposite direction, and why they were both so silent.

The children stood in the road, watching the wagon as long as they could see it, but Nick had slunk away into the woods. He could not bear the sight of their grief. He walked on, hardly knowing where he went. He felt as if he were trying to get rid of himself. He appreciated fully now the consequences of what he had done. Barney, innocent Barney, would be thrust into jail.

He began to see that the most terrible phase of moral cowardice is its capacity to injure others, and he could not endure the thought of what he had brought upon his friend.

Soon he was saying to himself that something was sure to happen to prevent them from putting Barney in prison, — he should n't be surprised if it were to happen before the wagon could reach the foot of the mountain.

In his despair, he had flung himself at length upon the rugged, stony ground at the base of a great crag. When this comforting thought of Barney's release came upon him, he took his hands from his face, and looked about him. From certain ledges of the cliff above, the road which led down the valley was visible at intervals for some distance. There he could watch the progress of the wagon, and see for a time longer what was happening to Barney.

There was a broad gulf between the wall of the mountain and the crag, which, from its detached position and its shape, was known far and wide as the "Old Man's Chimney."

It loomed up like a great stone column, a hundred feet above the wooded slope where Nick stood, and its height could only be ascended by dexterous climbing.

He went at it like a cat. Sometimes he helped himself up by sharp projections of the rock, sometimes by slipping his feet and hands into crevices, and sometimes he caught hold of a strong bush here and there, and gave himself a lift. When he was about forty feet from the base, he sat down on one of the ledges, and turning, looked anxiously along the red clay road which he could see winding among the trees down the mountain's side.

No wagon was there.

His eyes followed the road further and further toward the foot of the range, and then along the valley beyond. There, at least two miles distant, was a small moving black object, plainly defined upon the red clay of the road.

Barney was gone! There was no mistake about it. They had taken him away from Goliath Mountain! He was innocent, and Nick knew it, and Nick had made him seem guilty. There was no one near him now to speak a good word for him, not even his palsied old grandmother.

It all came back upon Nick with a rush.

His eyes were blurred with rising tears. Unconsciously, in his grief, he made a movement forward, and suddenly clutched convulsively at the ledge.

He had lost his balance. There was a swift, fantastic whirl of vague objects before him, then a great light seemed flashing through his very brain, and he knew that he was falling.

He knew nothing else for some time. He wondered where he was when he first opened his eyes and saw the great stone shaft towering high above, and the tops of the sun-gilded maples waving about him.

Then he remembered and understood. He had fallen from that narrow ledge, hardly ten feet above his head, and had been caught in his descent by the far broader one upon which he lay.

"It knocked the senses out'n me fur a while, I reckon," he said to himself. "But I hev toler'ble luck now, sure ez shootin', kase I mought hev drapped over this ledge, an' then I 'd hev been gone fur sartain sure!"

His exultation was short-lived. What was this limp thing hanging to his shoulder? and what was this thrill of pain darting through it?

He looked at it in amazement. It was his strong right arm — broken — helpless.

And here he was, perched thirty feet above the earth, weakened by his long faint, sore and bruised and unnerved by his fall, and with only his left arm to aid him in making that perilous descent.

It was impossible. He glanced down at the sheer walls of the column below, shook his head, and lay back on the ledge. Reckless as he was, he realized that the attempt would be fatal.

Then came a thought that filled him with dismay, -- how long was this to last? — who would rescue him?

He knew that a prolonged absence from home would create no surprise. His mother would only fancy that he had slipped off, as he had often done, to go on a camp-hunt with some other boys. She would not grow uneasy for a week, at least.

He was deep in the heart of the forest, distant from any dwelling. No one, as far as he knew, came to this spot, except himself and Barney, and their errand here was for the sake of the exhilaration and the hazard of climbing the crag. It was so lonely that on the Old Man's Chimney the eagles built instead of the swallows. His hope — his only hope — was that some hunter might chance to pass before he should die of hunger.

The shadow of the great obelisk shifted as the day wore on, and left him in the broad, hot glare of the sun. His broken arm was fevered and gave him great pain. Now and then he raised himself on the other, and looked down wistfully at the cool, dusky depths of the woods. He heard continually the impetuous rushing of a mountain torrent near at hand; sometimes, when the wind stirred the foliage, he caught a glimpse of the water, rioting from rock to rock, and he was oppressed by an intolerable thirst.

Thus the hours lagged wearily on.

CHAPTER IV

When the wagon was rolling along the road in the valley, Barney at first kept his eyes persistently fastened upon the craggy heights and the red and gold autumnal woods of Goliath Mountain, as the mighty range stretched across the plain.

But presently the two men began to talk to him, and he turned around in order to face them. They were urging him to confess his own guilt and tell who were the other burglars, and where they were. But Barney had nothing to tell. He could only protest again and again his innocence. The men, however, shook their heads incredulously, and after a while they left him to himself and smoked their pipes in silence.

When Barney looked back at the mountains once more, a startling change seemed to have been wrought in the landscape. Instead of the frowning sandstone cliffs he loved so well, and the gloomy recesses of the woods, there was only a succession of lines of a delicate blue color drawn along the horizon. This was the way the distant ranges looked from the crags of his own home; he knew that they were the mountains, but which was Goliath?

Suddenly he struck his hands together, and broke out with a bitter cry.

" I hev los' G'liath ! " he exclaimed. " I dunno whar I live ! An' whar *is* Melissy ? "

A difficult undertaking, certainly, to determine where among all those great spurs and outliers, stretching so far on either hand, was that little atom of dimpled pink-and-white humanity known as " Melissy."

The constable, being a native of these hills himself, knew something by experience of the homesickness of an exiled mountaineer, — far more terrible than the homesickness of lowlanders ; he took his pipe promptly from between his lips, and told the boy that the second blue ridge, counting down from the sky, was " G'liath Mounting," and that " Melissy war right thar somewhar."

Barney looked back at it with unrecogniz-

ing eyes, — this gentle, misty, blue vagueness
was not the solemn, sombre mountain that he
knew. He gazed at it only for a moment
longer; then his heart swelled and he burst
into tears.

On and on they went through the flat
country. The boy felt that he could scarcely
breathe. Even tourists, coming down from
these mountains to the valley below, struggle
with a sense of suffocation and oppression;
how must it have been then with this half-
wild creature, born and bred on those breezy
heights!

The stout mules did their duty well, and it
was not long before they were in sight of the
cross-roads store that had been robbed. It
was a part of a small frame dwelling-house,
set in the midst of the yellow sunlight that
brooded over the plain. All the world around
it seemed to the young backwoodsman to be
a big cornfield; but there was a garden close
at hand, and tall sunflowers looked over the
fence and seemed to nod knowingly at Barney, as much as to say they had always sus-

pected him of being one of the burglars,
and were gratified that he had been caught
at last.

Poor fellow! he saw so much suspicion
expressed in the faces of a crowd of men
congregating about the store, that it was no
wonder he fancied he detected it too in inani-
mate objects.

Of all the group only one seemed to doubt
his guilt. He overheard Blenkins, the mer-
chant, say to Jim Dow, —

"It's mighty hard to b'lieve this story on
this 'ere boy ; he 's a manly looking, straight-
for'ard little chap, an' he 's got honest eyes
in his head, too."

"He 'd a deal better hev an honest heart
in his body," drawled Jim Dow, who was
convinced that Barney had aided in the
burglary.

When they had gone around to the window
with the broken pane, Barney looked up at it
in great anxiety. If only it should prove too
small for him to slip through ! Certainly it
seemed very small.

He had pulled off his coat and stood ready to jump.

" Up with you ! " said Stebbins.

The boy laid both hands on the sill, gave a light spring, and went through the pane like an eel.

" That settles it ! " he heard Stebbins saying outside. And all the idlers were laughing because it was done so nimbly.

" That boy 's right smart of a fool," said one of the lookers-on. "Now, if that had been me, I 'd hev made out to git stuck somehows in that winder ; I 'd have scotched my wheel somewhere."

" Ef ye hed, I 'd have dragged ye through ennyhow," declared Jim Dow, who had no toleration of a joke on a serious subject. " This hyar boy air a deal too peart ter try enny sech fool tricks on *Me !* "

Barney hardly knew how he got back into the wagon ; he only knew that they were presently jolting along once more in the midst of the yellow glare of sunlight. It had begun to seem that there was no chance for him.

Like Nick, he too had madly believed, in spite of everything, that something would happen to help him. He could not think that, innocent as he was, he would be imprisoned. Now, however, this fate evidently was very close upon him.

Suddenly Jim Dow spoke. " I s'pose ye war powerful disapp'inted kase ye could n't git yerself hitched in that thar winder; ye air too well used to it, — ye hev been through it afore."

" I hev never been through it afore ! " cried Barney indignantly.

" Well, well," said Stebbins pacifically, " it would n't have done you any good if you had n't gone through the pane just now. I'd have only thought you were one of those who stood on the outside. You see, the *main* point against you is that scrap of your coat and your button found right there by the Conscripts' Hollow, — though, of course, your going through the window-pane so easy makes it more complete."

Barney's tired brain began to fumble at this problem, — how did it happen?

He had not been on the ledge nor at the Conscripts' Hollow for six months at least. Yet there was that bit of his coat and his button found on the bush close at hand only to-day.

Was it possible that he could have exchanged coats by mistake with Nick the last afternoon that they were on the crag together?

"Did Nick wear *my* coat down on the ledge, I wonder, an' git it tored? Did Nick see the plunder in the Conscripts' Hollow, an' git skeered, an' then sot out ter lyin' ter git shet o' the blame?"

As he asked himself these questions, he began to remember, vaguely, having seen, just as he was falling asleep, his friend's head slowly disappearing beneath the verge of the crag.

"Nick started down ter the ledge, anyhow," he argued.

Did he dream it, or was it true, that when Nick came back he seemed at first strangely agitated?

All at once Barney exclaimed aloud, —

"This hyar air a powerful cur'ous thing 'bout'n that thar piece what war tored out'n my coat!"

"What's curious about it?" asked Stebbins quickly.

Jim Dow took his pipe from his mouth, and looked sharply at the boy.

Barney struggled for a moment with a strong temptation. Then a nobler impulse asserted itself. He would not even attempt to shield himself behind the friend who had done him so grievous an injury.

He *knew* nothing positively; he must not put his suspicions and his vague, half-sleeping impressions into words, and thus possibly criminate Nick.

He himself felt certain now how the matter really stood, — that Nick had no connection whatever with the robbery, but having accidentally stumbled upon the stolen goods, he had become panic-stricken, had lied about it, and finally had saved himself at the expense of an innocent friend.

Still, Barney had no *proof* of this, and he felt he would rather suffer unjustly himself than unjustly throw blame on another.

"Nothin', nothin'," he said absently. "I war jes' a-studyin' 'bout'n it all."

"Well, I would n't think about it any more just now," said good-natured Stebbins. "You look like you had been dragged through a keyhole instead of a window-pane. This town we 're coming to is the biggest town you ever saw."

Barney could not respond to this attempt to divert his attention. He could only brood upon the fact that he was innocent, and would be punished as if he were guilty, and that it was Nick Gregory, his chosen friend, who had brought him to this pass.

He would not be unmanly, and injure Nick with a possibly unfounded suspicion, but his heart burned with indignation and contempt when he thought of him. He felt that he would go through fire and water to be justly revenged upon him.

He determined that, if ever he should see

Nick again, even though years might intervene, he would tax him with the injury he had wrought, and make him answer for it.

Barney clenched his fists as he looked back at the ethereal blue shadows that they said were the solid old hills.

Perhaps, however, if he had known where, in the misty uncertainty that enveloped Goliath Mountain, Nick Gregory was at this moment, — far away in the lonely woods, helpless with his broken arm, perched high up on the " Old Man's Chimney," — Barney might have thought himself the more fortunately placed of the two.

Before he was well aware of it, the wagon was jolting into the town. He took no notice of how much larger the little village was than any he had ever seen before. His attention was riveted by the faces of the people who ran to the doors and windows, upon recognizing the officers, to stare at him as one of the burglars.

When the wagon reached the public square, a number of men came up and stopped it.

Barney was surprised that they took so little notice of him. They were talking loudly and excitedly to the officers, who grew at once loud and excited, too.

The boy roused himself, and began to listen to the conversation. The burglars had been captured! — yes, that was what they were saying. The deputy-sheriff had nabbed the whole gang in a western district of the county this morning early, and they were lodged at this moment in jail. Barney's heart sank. Would he be put among the guilty creatures? He flinched from the very idea.

Suddenly, here was the deputy-sheriff himself, a young man, dusty and tired with his long, hard ride, but with an air of great satisfaction in his success. He talked with many quick gestures that were very expressive. Sometimes he would leave a sentence unfinished except by a brisk nod, but all the crowd caught its meaning instantly. This peculiarity gave him a very animated manner, and he seemed to Barney to enjoy being in a position of authority.

He pressed his foaming horse close to the wagon, and leaning over, looked searchingly into Barney's face.

The poor boy looked up deprecatingly from under his limp and drooping hat-brim.

All the crowd stood in silence, watching them. After a moment of this keen scrutiny, the deputy turned to the constable with an interrogative wave of the hand.

"This hyar's the boy what war put through the winder-pane ter thieve from Blenkins," said Jim Dow. "Thar's consider'ble fac's agin him."

"You mean well, Jim," said the deputy, with a short, scornful laugh. "But your performance ain't always equal to your intentions."

He lifted his eyebrows and nodded in a significant way that the crowd understood, for there was a stir of excitement in its midst; but poor Barney failed to catch his meaning. He hung upon every tone and gesture with the intensest interest. All the talk was about him, and he could comprehend no more than if the man spoke in a foreign language.

Still, he gathered something of the drift of the speech from the constable's reply.

"That thar boy's looks hev bamboozled more 'n one man ter-day, jes' at fust," Jim Dow drawled. "*Looks* ain't nothin'."

"I'd believe 'most anything a boy with a face on him like that would tell me," said the deputy. "And besides, you see, one of those scamps," with a quick nod toward the jail, "has turned State's evidence."

Barney's heart was in a great tumult. It seemed bursting. There was a hot rush of blood to his head. He was dizzy — and he could not understand!

State's evidence, — what was that? and what would that do to him?

CHAPTER V

Barney observed that these words produced a marked sensation. The crowd began to press more closely around the deputy-sheriff's foaming horse.

"Who hev done turned State's evidence?" asked Jim Dow.

"Little Jeff Carew, — you've seen that puny little man a-many a time — have n't you, Jim? He'd go into your pocket."

"He would, I know, powerful quick, ef he thunk I hed ennything in it," said Jim, with a gruff laugh.

"I did n't mean that, though it's true enough. I only went ter say that he's small enough to go into any ordinary-sized fellow's pocket. Some of the rest of them wanted to turn State's evidence, but they were n't allowed. They were harder customers even than Jeff Carew, — regular old jail-birds."

Barney began to vaguely understand that when a prisoner confesses the crime he has committed, and gives testimony which will convict his partners in it, this is called turning "State's evidence."

But how was it to concern Barney?

An old white-haired man had pushed up to the wagon; he polished his spectacles on his coat-tail, then put them on his nose, and focused them on Barney. Those green spectacles seemed to the boy to have a solemnly accusing expression on their broad and sombre lenses. He shrank as the old man spoke, —

"And is this the boy who was slipped through the window to steal from Blenkins?"

"No," said the deputy, "this ain't the boy."

Barney could hardly believe his senses.

"Fact is," continued the deputy, with a brisk wave of his hand, "there was n't any boy with 'em, — so little Jeff Carew says. *He* jumped through the window-pane *himself*. We would n't believe that until we measured one there at the jail of the same size as Blenkins's window-glass, and he went through it without a wriggle."

Barney sprang to his feet.

"Oh, tell it ter me, folkses!" he cried wildly; "tell it ter me, somebody! Will they keep me hyar all the same? An' when will I see G'liath Mounting agin, an' be whar Melissy air?"

He had burst into tears, and there was a murmur of sympathy in the crowd.

"Oh, that lets you out, I reckon, youngster," said Stebbins. " I 'm glad enough of it for one."

The old man turned his solemnly accusing green spectacles on Stebbins, and it seemed to Barney that he spoke with no less solemnly accusing a voice.

" He ought never to have been let in."

Stebbins replied, rather eagerly, Barney thought, " Why, there was enough against that boy to have clapped him in jail, and maybe convicted him, if this man had n't turned State's evidence."

" We hed the fac's agin him, — dead agin him," chimed in Jim Dow.

" That just shows how much danger an innocent boy was in ; it seems to me that somebody ought to have been more careful," the old man protested.

" That 's so ! " came in half a dozen voices from the crowd.

Barney was surprised to see how many friends he had now, when a moment before he had had none. But he ought to have realized that there is a great difference between *being* a young martyr, and *seeming* a young thief.

" I want to see the little fellow out of this," said the old man with the terrible spectacles.

He saw him out of it in a short while.

There was an examination before a magistrate, in which Barney was discharged on the testimony of Jeff Carew, who was produced and swore that he had never before seen the boy, that he was not among the gang of burglars who had robbed Blenkins's store and dwelling-house, and that he had had no part in helping to conceal the plunder. In opposition to this, the mere finding of a scrap of Barney's coat close to the Conscripts' Hollow seemed now of slight consequence, although it could not be accounted for.

When the trial was over, the old man with the green spectacles took Barney to his house, gave him something to eat, and saw him start out homeward.

As Barney plodded along toward the blue mountains his heart was very bitter against Nick Gregory, who had lied and thrown suspicion upon him and brought him into danger. Whenever he thought of it he raised

his clenched fist and shook it. He was a
little fellow, but he felt that with the strength
of this grievance he was more than a match
for big Nick Gregory. He would force him
to confess the lies that he had told and his
cowardice, and all Goliath Mountain should
know it and despise him for it.

"I'll fetch an' kerry that word to an' fro
fur a thousand mile!" Barney declared between his set teeth.

Now and then a wagoner overtook him and
gave him a ride, thus greatly helping him on
his way. As he went, there was a gradual
change in the blue and misty range that
seemed to encircle the west, and which he
knew, by one deep indentation in the horizontal line of its summit, was Goliath Mountain.
It became first an intenser blue. As he drew
nearer still, it turned a bronzed green. It
had purpled with the sunset before he could
distinguish the crimson and gold of its foliage
and its beetling crags. Night had fallen when
he reached the base of the mountain.

There was no moon; heavy clouds were

rolling up from the horizon, and they hid the stars. Nick Gregory, lying on the ledge of the "Old Man's Chimney," thirty feet above the black earth, could not see his hand before his face. The darkness was dreadful to him. It had closed upon a dreadful day. The seconds were measured by the throbs and dartings of pain in his arm. He was almost exhausted by hunger and thirst. He thought, however, that he could have borne it all cheerfully, but for the sharp remorse that tortured him for the wrong he had done to his friend, and his wild anxiety about Barney's fate. Nick felt that he, himself, was on trial here, imprisoned on this tower of stone, cut off from the world, from everything but his sternly accusing conscience and his guilty heart.

For hours he had heard nothing but the monotonous rushing of the water close at hand, or now and then the shrill, quavering cry of a distant screech-owl, or the almost noiseless flapping of a bat's wings as they swept by him.

He had hardly a hope of deliverance, when suddenly there came a new sound, vague and indistinguishable. He lifted himself upon his left elbow and listened again. He could hear nothing for a moment except his own panting breath and the loud beating of his heart. But there — the sound came once more. What was it? a dropping leaf? the falling of a fragment of stone from the " Chimney "? a distant step ?

It grew more distinct as it drew nearer ; presently he recognized it, — the regular footfall of some man or boy plodding along the path. That path ! — a recollection flashed through his mind. No one knew that short cut up the mountain but him and Barney; they had worn the path with their trampings back and forth from the " Old Man's Chimney."

He thought he must be dreaming, or that he had lost his reason ; still he shouted out, " Hold on, thar ! air it ye, Barney ? "

The step paused. Then a reply came in a voice that he hardly recognized as Barney's ;

it was so fierce, and so full of half-repressed anger.

"Yes, it air Barney,—ef *ye* hev any call ter know."

"How did ye git away, Barney?—how did ye git away?" exclaimed Nick, with a joyous sense of relief.

"A *thief's* word cl'ared me!"

This bitter cry came up to Nick, sharp and distinct, through the dark stillness. He said nothing at the moment, and presently he heard Barney speak again, as he stood invisible, and enveloped in the gloom of the night, at the foot of the mighty column.

"'T war my bes' frien' ez sunk me deep in trouble. But the *thief,* he fished me up. He 'lowed ter the jestice ez I never holped him ter steal nothin' nor ter hide it arterward, nuther."

Nick said not a word. The hot tears came into his eyes. Barney, he thought, could feel no more bitterly toward him than he felt toward himself.

"How kem my coat ter be tored down thar

on the ledge, close ter the Conscripts' Hollow, whar I hain't been sence the cloth war wove ?"

There was a long pause.

" I wore it thar, Barney, 'stid o' mine," Nick replied at last. " I never knowed, at fust, ez I hed tored it. I was so skeered when I seen the stole truck, I never knowed nothin'."

" An' then ye spoke a lie ! An' arterward, ye let the folks think ez 't war me ez hed tored that coat close by the Conscripts' Hollow ! "

" I was skeered haffen ter death, Barney !"

Nick was very contemptible in his falsehood and cowardice, — even in his repentance and shame and sorrow. At least, so the boy thought who stood in the darkness at the foot of the great column. Suddenly it occurred to Barney that this was a strange place for Nick to be at this hour of the night. His indignation gave way for a moment to some natural curiosity.

" What air ye a-doin' of up thar on the Old Man's Chimney ? " he asked.

"I kem up hyar this mornin' early, ter watch the wagon a-takin' ye off. Then I fell and bruk my arm, an' I can't git down 'thout bein' holped a little."

There was another silence, so intense that it seemed to Nick as if he were all alone again in the immensity of the mountains, and the black night, and the endless forests. He had expected an immediate proffer of assistance from Barney. He had thought that his injured friend would relent in his severity when he knew that he had suffered too; that he was in great pain even at this moment.

But not a word came from Barney.

"I hed laid off ter ax ye ter holp me a little," Nick faltered meekly, making his appeal direct.

There was no answer.

It was so still that the boy, high up on the sandstone pillar, could hear the wind rising among the far spurs west of Goliath. The foliage near at hand was ominously quiet in the sultry air. Once there was a flash of lightning from the black clouds, followed by a low muttering of thunder. Then all was still again, — so still!

Nick raised himself upon his left arm, and leaned cautiously over the verge of the ledge, peering, with starting eyes, into the darkness, and hoping for another flash of lightning that he might see below for an instant. A terrible suspicion had come to him. Could Barney have slipped quietly away, leaving him to his fate?

He could see nothing in the impenetrable gloom; he could hear nothing in the dark stillness.

Barney had not yet gone, but he was saying to himself, as he stood at the foot of the great obelisk, that here was his revenge, far more complete than he had dared even to hope.

He could measure out his false friend's punishment in any degree he thought fit. He could leave him there with his broken arm and his pangs of hunger for another day. He deserved it, — he deserved it richly. The recollection was still very bitter to Barney of the hardships he had endured at the hands of this boy, who asked him now for help. Why did he not refuse it? Why should he not take the revenge he had promised himself?

And then he knew there was danger in now trying to climb the jagged edges of the Old Man's Chimney. His nerves were shaken by the excitements of the day; he was fagged out by his long tramp; the wind was beginning to surge among the trees; it might blow him from his uncertain foothold. But when it gained more strength, might it not drive Nick, helpless with his broken arm, from that high ledge?

As this thought crossed his mind, he tore off his hat, coat, and shoes, and desperately began the ascent. He thought he knew every projection and crevice and bush so well that he might have found his way blindfolded, and guided by the sense of touch alone. But he did not lack for light. Before he was six feet up from the ground, the clouds were rent by a vivid flash, and an instantaneous peal of thunder woke all the echoes. This was the breaking of the storm; afterward, there was a continuous pale flickering over all the sky, and at close intervals, dazzling gleams of lightning darted through the rain, which was now falling heavily.

"I 'm a-comin', Nick!" shouted Barney, through the din of the elements.

Somehow, as he climbed, he felt light-hearted again. It seemed to him that he had left a great weight at the foot of the gigantic sandstone column. Could it be that bitter revenge he had promised himself? He had thought only of Nick's safety, but he seemed to have done himself a kindness in forgiving his friend, — the burden of revenge is so heavy! His troubles were already growing faint in his memory, — it was so good to feel the rain splashing in his face, and his rude playfellow, the mountain wind, rioting around him once more. He was laughing when at last he pulled himself up, wet through and through, on the ledge beside Nick.

" It 's airish up hyar, ain't it? " he cried.

" Barney," said Nick miserably, " I dunno how I kin ever look at ye agin, squar' in the face, while I lives."

"Shet that up ! " Barney returned good-humoredly. " I don't want ter ever hear 'bout'n it no more. I 'll always know, arter this, that I can't place no dependence in ye ; but, law, ye air jes' like that old gun o' mine ; sometimes it 'll hang fire, an' sometimes it 'll go off at half-cock, an' ginerally it disapp'ints me mightily. But, somehows, I can't deter-minate to shoot with no other one. I 'll hev ter feel by ye jes' like I does by that thar old gun."

The descent was slow and difficult, and very painful to Nick, and fraught with con-siderable danger to both boys. They accom-plished it in safety, however, and then, with Barney's aid, Nick managed to drag himself through the woods to the nearest log cabin, where his arm was set by zealous and sympa-thetic amateurs in a rude fashion that probably would have shocked the faculty. They had some supper here, and an invitation to remain all night; but Barney was wild to be at home, and Nick, in his adversity, clung to his friend.

The rain had ceased, and they had only half a mile further to go. Barney's heart was exultant when he saw the light in the window of his home, and the sparks flying up from the chimney. He had some curiosity to know how the family circle looked without him.

"Ye wait hyar, Nick, a minute, an' I'll take a peek at 'em afore I bounce in 'mongst 'em," he said. "I'm all eat up ter know what Melissy air a-doin' 'thout me."

But the sight smote the tears from his eyes when he stole around to the window and glanced in at the little group, plainly shown in the flare from the open fire.

Granny looked ten years older since morning. The three small boys, instead of popping corn or roasting apples and sweet potatoes, as was their habit in the evenings, sat in a dismal row, their chins on their freckled, sunburned hands, and their elbows on their knees, and gazed ruefully at the fire. And

Melissy, — why, there was Melissy, a little blue-and-white ball curled up on the floor. Asleep? No. Barney caught the gleam of her wide-open blue eyes; but he missed something from them, — the happy expression that used to dwell there.

He went at the door with a rush. And what an uproar there was when he suddenly sprang in among them! Melissy laughed until she cried. Granny whirled and whirled her stick, and nodded convulsively, and gasped out eager questions about the trial and the "jedge." The little boys jumped for joy until they seemed strung on wire.

Soon they were popping corn and roasting apples once more. The flames roared up the chimney, and the shadows danced on the wall, and as the hours wore on, they were all so happy that when midnight came, it caught them still grouped around the fire.

A WARNING

It was night on Elm Ridge. So black, so black that the great crags and chasms were hidden, the forest was lost in the encompassing gloom, the valley and the distant ranges were gone, — all the world had disappeared.

There was no wind, and the dark clouds above the dark earth hung low and motionless. Solomon Grow found it something of an undertaking to grope his way back from the little hut of unhewn logs, where he had stabled his father's horse, to the door of the cabin and the home-circle within.

He fumbled for the latchstring, and pulling it carelessly, the door flew open suddenly, and he almost fell into the room.

"Why d' ye come a-bustin' in hyar that thar way, Sol?" his mother demanded rather tartly. "Ef ye hed been raised 'mongst the foxes, ye could n't show less manners."

"Door slipped out'n my hand," said Sol, a trifle sullenly.

"Waal — air ye disabled anywhar so ez ye can't shet it, eh?" asked his father, with a touch of sarcasm.

Sol shut the door, drew up an inverted tub, seated himself upon it, and looked about, loweringly. He thought he had been needlessly affronted. Still, he held his peace.

Within, there was a great contrast to the black night outside. The ash and hickory logs in the deep fireplace threw blue and yellow flames high up the wide stone chimney. The flickering light was like some genial, cheery smile forever coming and going.

It illumined the circle about the hearth. There sat Sol's mother, idle to-night, for it was Sunday. His grandmother, too, was there, so old that she seemed to confirm the story told of these healthy mountains, to the effect that people are obliged to go down in the valley to die, else they would live forever.

There was Sol's father, a great burly fellow, six feet three inches in height, still holding

out his hands to the blaze, chilled through
and through by his long ride from the church
where he had been to hear the circuit-rider
preach on " Forgiveness of Injuries."

He was beginning now to quarrel vehemently with his brother-in-law, Jacob Smith,
about the shabby treatment he had recently
experienced in the non-payment of work, —
for work in this country is a sort of circulat-
ing medium ; a man will plough a day for
another man, on condition that the favor is
rigorously reciprocated.

Jacob Smith had been to the still, and ap-
parently had imbibed the spirit there prevail-
ing, to more effect than Sol's father had
absorbed the spirit that had been taught in
church.

In plain words, Jacob Smith was very
drunk, and very quarrelsome, and very unreasonable. The genial firelight that played
upon his bloated face played also over objects
much pleasanter to look upon, — over the
strings of red pepper-pods hanging from the
rafters ; over the bright variegations of color

in the clean patchwork quilt on the bed; over the shining pans and pails set aside on the shelf; over the great, curious frame of the warping-bars, rising up among the shadows on the other side of the room, the equidistant pegs still holding the sized yarn that Solomon's mother had been warping, preparatory to weaving.

On the other side of the room, too, was a little tow-headed child sitting in a cradle, which, small as he was, he had long ago outgrown as a bed.

It was only a pine box placed upon rude rockers, and he used it for a rocking-chair. His bare, fat legs hung out on one side of the box, and as he delightedly rocked back and forth, his grotesque little shadow waved to and fro on the wall, and mocked and flouted him.

What he thought of it, nobody can ever know; his grave eyes were fixed upon it, but he said nothing, and the silent shadow and substance swayed joyously hither and thither together.

The quarrel between the two men was becoming hot and bitter. One might have expected nothing better from Jacob Smith, for when a man is drunk, the human element drops like a husk, and only the unreasoning brute is left.

But had John Grow forgotten all the good words he had heard to-day from the circuit-rider? Had they melted into thin air during his long ride from the church? Were the houseless good words wandering with the rising wind through the unpeopled forest, seeking vainly a human heart where they might find a lodgment?

The men had risen from their chairs; the drunkard, tremulous with anger, had drawn a sharp knife. John Grow was not so patient as he might have been, considering the great advantage he had in being sober, and the good words with which he had started out from the " meet'n'-house."

He laid his heavy hand angrily upon the drunken man's shoulder.

In another moment there would have been

bloodshed. But suddenly the dark shadows at the other end of the room swayed with a strange motion; a great creaking sound arose, and the warping-bars tottered forward and fell upon the floor with a crash.

The wranglers turned with anxious faces. No one was near the bars, it seemed that naught could have jarred them; but there lay the heavy frame upon the floor, the pegs broken, and the yarn twisted.

"A warning!" cried Sol's mother. "A warning how you-uns spen' the evenin' o' the Lord's Day in yer quar'lin', an' fightin', an' sech. An' ye, John Grow, jes' from the meet'n'-house!"

She did not reproach her brother, — nobody hopes anything from a drunkard.

"A sign o' bad luck," said the grandmother. "It 'minds me o' the time las' winter that the wind blowed the door in, an' straight arter that the cow died."

"Them signs air ez likely ter take hold on folks ez on cattle," said Jacob Smith, half-sobered by the shock.

There was a look of sudden anxiety on the face of Solomon's mother. She crossed the room to the youngster rocking in the cradle.

"Come, Benny," she said, " ye oughter go ter bed. Ye air wastin' yer strength sittin' up this late in the night. An' ye war a-coughin' las' week. Ye must go ter bed."

Benny clung to his unique rocking-chair with a sturdy strength which promised well for his muscle when he should be as old as his great, strong brother Solomon. He had been as quiet, hitherto, as if he were dumb, but now he lifted up his voice in a loud and poignant wail, and after he was put to bed, he resurrected himself from among the bedclothes, ever and anon, with a bitter, though infantile, jargon of protest.

"I'm fairly afeard o' them bars," said Mrs. Grow, looking down upon the prostrate timbers. "It's comical that they fell down that-a-way. I hopes 't ain't no sign o' bad luck. I would n't hev nothin' ter happen fur nothin'. An' Benny war a-coughin' las' week."

She had not even the courage to put her

fear into words. And she tenderly admonished tow-headed Benny, who was once more getting out of bed, to go to sleep and save his strength, and remember how he was coughing last week.

"He hed a chicken-bone acrost his throat," said his father. "No wonder he coughed."

Solomon rose and went out into the black night, — so black that he could not distinguish the sky from the earth, or the unobstructed air from the dense forest around.

He walked about blindly, dragging something heavily after him. The weight of concealment it was. He knew something that nobody knew besides.

At the critical moment of the altercation, he had stepped softly among the shadows to the warping-bars, — a strong push had sent the great frame crashing down. He was back in an instant among the others, and by reason of the excitement his agency in the sensation was not detected.

Like his biblical namesake, Solomon was no fool. Had he been reared in a cultivated community, with the advantages of education, he might have been one of the bright young fellows who manage other young fellows, who control debating societies, who are prominent in mysterious associations, the secret of which is at once guarded and represented by a Cerberus of three Greek letters.

But, wise as he was, Solomon was not a prophet. He had intended only to effect a diversion, and stop the quarrel. He had had no prevision of the panic of superstition that he had raised in the minds of these simple people ; for the ignorant mountaineer is a devout believer in signs and warnings.

As Solomon wandered about outside, he heard his father stumbling from the door of the house to the barn to see if aught of evil had come to the cow or the horse. He knew how his grandmother's heart was wrung with fear for her heifer, and he could hardly endure to think of his mother's anxieties about Benny.

No prophetic eye was needed to foresee the terrors that would beset her in the days to come, when she would walk back and forth before the bars, warping the yarn to be woven into cloth for his and Benny's clothes; how she would regard the harmless frame as an uncanny thing, endowed with supernatural powers, and look askance at it, and shrink from touching it; how she would watch for the sign to come true, and tremble lest it come.

He turned about, dragging and tugging this weight of concealment after him, reëntered the house, and sat down beside the fire.

His uncle Jacob Smith had gone to his own home. The others were telling stories, calculated to make one's hair stand on end, about signs and warnings, and their horrible fulfillment.

" Granny," said Solomon suddenly.

" Waal, sonny ? " said his grandmother.

When the eyes of the family group were fixed upon him, Solomon's courage failed.

" Nothin'," he said hastily. " Nothin' at all."

" Why, what ails the boy ? " exclaimed his mother.

"I tell ye now, Solomon," said his grandmother, with an emphatic nod, "ye hed better respec' yer elders, — an' a sign in the house!"

Solomon slept little that night. Toward day he began to dream of the warping-bars. They seemed to develop suddenly into an immense animated monster, from which he only escaped by waking with a sudden start.

Then he found that a great white morning, full of snow, was breaking upon the black night. And what a world it was now! The mountain was graced with a soft white drapery; on every open space there were vague suggestions of delicate colors: in this hollow lay a tender purple shadow; on that steep slope was an elusive roseate flush, and when you looked again, it was gone, and the glare was blinding.

The bare black branches of the trees formed strangely interlaced hieroglyphics upon the turquoise sky. The crags were dark and grim, despite their snowy crests and the gigantic glittering icicles that here and there depended from them. A cascade, close by in the gorge, had been stricken motionless and dumb, as if by a sudden spell; and still and silent, it sparkled in the sun.

The snow lay deep on the roof of the log cabin, and the eaves were decorated with shining icicles. The enchantment had followed the zigzag lines of the fence, and on every rail was its embellishing touch.

All the homely surroundings were transfigured. The potato-house was a vast white billow, the ash-hopper was a marble vase, and the fodder-stack was a great conical ermine cap, belonging to some mountain giant who had lost it in the wind last night.

"I mought hev knowed that we-uns war a-goin' ter hev this spell o' weather by the sign o' the warpin'-bars fallin' las' night," said John Grow, stamping off the snow as he came in from feeding his horse.

"I hope 't ain't no worse sign," said his wife. "But I misdoubts." And she sighed heavily.

"'T ain't no sign at all," said Solomon

suddenly. He could keep his secret no longer. "'T war me ez flung down them warpin'-bars."

For a moment they all stared at him in silent amazement.

"What fur?" demanded his father at last. "Just ter enjye sottin' 'em up agin? I'll teach ye ter fling down warpin'-bars!"

"Waal," said the peacemaker, hesitating, "it 'peared ter me ez Uncle Jacob Smith war toler'ble drunk, — take him all tergether, — an' ez he hed drawed a knife, I thought that ye an' him hed 'bout quar'led enough. An' so I flung down the warpin'-bars ter git the fuss shet up."

"Waal, sir!" exclaimed his grandmother, red with wrath. "Ez ef *my* son could n't stand up agin all the Smiths that ever stepped! Ye must fling down the warpin'-bars an' twist the spun-truck — fur Jacob Smith!"

"Look-a-hyar, Sol," said his father gruffly, "'tend ter yerself, an' yer own quar'ls, arter this, will ye!"

Then, with a sudden humorous interpretation of the incident, he broke into a guffaw.

" I hev lived a consider'ble time in this tantalizin' world, an' ez yit I dunno ez I hev hed any need o' Sol ter pertect *me*."

But Sol had unburdened his mind, and felt at ease again ; not the less because he knew that but for his novel method of making peace, there might have been something worse than a sign in the house.

It was a critical moment. There was a stir other than that of the wind among the pine needles and dry leaves that carpeted the ground.

The wary wild turkeys lifted their long necks with that peculiar cry of half-doubting surprise so familiar to a sportsman, then all was still for an instant.

The world was steeped in the noontide sunlight, the mountain air tasted of the fresh sylvan fragrance that pervaded the forest, the foliage blazed with the red and gold of autumn, the distant Chilhowee heights were delicately blue.

That instant's doubt sealed the doom of one of the flock. As the turkeys stood in momentary suspense, the sunlight gilding their bronze feathers to a brighter sheen, there was a movement in the dense undergrowth. The

flock took suddenly to wing, — a flash from
among the leaves, the sharp crack of a rifle,
and one of the birds fell heavily over the bluff
and down toward the valley.

The young mountaineer's exclamation of
triumph died in his throat. He came running to the verge of the crag, and looked
down ruefully into the depths where his
game had disappeared.

" Waal, sir," he broke forth pathetically,
" this beats my time ! If my luck ain't enough
ter make a horse laugh ! "

He did not laugh, however. Perhaps his
luck was calculated to stir only equine risi-
bility. The cliff was almost perpendicular; at
the depth of twenty feet a narrow ledge projected, but thence there was a sheer descent,
down, down, down, to the tops of the tall
trees in the valley far below.

As Ethan Tynes looked wistfully over the
precipice, he started with a sudden surprise.
There on the narrow ledge lay the dead
turkey.

The sight sharpened Ethan's regrets. He

had made a good shot, and he hated to relinquish his game. While he gazed in dismayed meditation, an idea began to kindle in his brain. Why could he not let himself down to the ledge by those long, strong vines that hung over the edge of the cliff?

It was risky, Ethan knew, — terribly risky. But then, — if only the vines were strong!

He tried them again and again with all his might, selected several of the largest, grasped them hard and fast, and then slipped lightly off the crag.

He waited motionless for a moment. His movements had dislodged clods of earth and fragments of rock from the verge of the cliff, and until these had ceased to rattle about his head and shoulders he did not begin his downward journey.

Now and then as he went he heard the snapping of twigs, and again a branch would break, but the vines which supported him were tough and strong to the last. Almost before he knew it he stood upon the ledge, and with a great sigh of relief he let the vines swing loose.

" Waal, that war n't sech a mighty job at last. But law, ef it hed been Peter Birt stid of me, that thar wild tur-r-key would hev laid on this hyar ledge plumb till the Jedgmint Day ! "

He walked deftly along the ledge, picked up the bird, and tied it to one of the vines with a string which he took from his pocket, intending to draw it up when he should be once more on the top of the crag. These preparations complete, he began to think of going back.

He caught the vines on which he had made the descent, but before he had fairly left the ledge, he felt that they were giving way.

He paused, let himself slip back to a secure foothold, and tried their strength by pulling with all his force.

Presently down came the whole mass in his hands. The friction against the sharp edges of the rock over which they had been stretched with a strong tension had worn them through. His first emotion was one of intense thankfulness that they had fallen while he was on the ledge instead of midway in his precarious ascent.

"Ef they hed kem down whilst I war a-goin' up, I 'd hev been flung plumb down ter the bottom o' the valley, 'kase this ledge air too narrer ter hev cotched me."

He glanced down at the sombre depths beneath. "Thar would n't hev been enough left of me ter pick up on a shovel!" he exclaimed, with a tardy realization of his foolish recklessness.

The next moment a mortal terror seized him. What was to be his fate? To regain the top of the cliff by his own exertions was an impossibility.

He cast his despairing eyes up the ascent, as sheer and as smooth as a wall, without a crevice which might afford a foothold, or a shrub to which he might cling.

His strong head was whirling as he again glanced downward to the unmeasured abyss beneath. He softly let himself sink into a sitting posture, his heels dangling over the

HOW LONG WAS IT TO LAST

frightful depths, and addressed himself resolutely to the consideration of the terrible danger in which he was placed.

Taken at its best, how long was it to last? Could he look to any human being for deliverance? He reflected with growing dismay that the place was far from any dwelling, and from the road that wound along the ridge.

There was no errand that could bring a man to this most unfrequented portion of the deep woods, unless an accident should hither direct some hunter's step.

It was quite possible, nay, probable, that years might elapse before the forest solitude would again be broken by human presence.

His brothers would search for him when he should be missed from home, — but such boundless stretches of forest! They might search for weeks and never come near this spot. He would die here, he would starve, — no, he would grow drowsy when exhausted and fall — fall — fall !

He was beginning to feel that morbid fascination that sometimes seizes upon those who stand on great heights, — an overwhelming impulse to plunge downward. His only salvation was to look up. He would look up to the sky.

And what were these words he was beginning to faintly remember? Had not the circuit-rider said in his last sermon that not even a sparrow falls to the ground unmarked of God? There was a definite strength in this suggestion. He felt less lonely as he stared resolutely at the big blue sky. There came into his heart a sense of encouragement, of hope.

He would keep up as long and as bravely as he could, and if the worst should come, — was he indeed so solitary? He would hold in remembrance the sparrow's fall.

He had so nerved himself to meet his fate that he thought it was a fancy when he heard a distant step. But it did not die away, it grew more and more distinct, — a shambling step, that curiously stopped at intervals and kicked the fallen leaves.

He sought to call out, but he seemed to have lost his voice. Not a sound issued from his thickened tongue and his dry throat. The step came nearer. It would presently pass. With a mighty effort Ethan sent forth a wild, hoarse cry.

The rocks reverberated it, the wind carried it far, and certainly there was an echo of its despair and terror in a shrill scream set up on the verge of the crag. Then Ethan heard the shambling step scampering off very fast indeed.

The truth flashed upon him. It was some child, passing on an unimaginable errand through the deep woods, frightened by his sudden cry.

"Stop, bubby!" he shouted; "stop a minute! It's Ethan Tynes that's callin' of ye. Stop a minute, bubby!"

The step paused at a safe distance, and the shrill pipe of a little boy demanded, "Whar is ye, Ethan Tynes?"

"I'm down hyar on the ledge o' the bluff. Who air ye ennyhow?"

"George Birt," promptly replied the little boy. "What air ye doin' down thar? I thought it war Satan a-callin' of me. I never seen nobody."

"I kem down hyar on vines arter a tur-r-key I shot. The vines bruk, an' I hev got no way ter git up agin. I want ye ter go ter yer mother's house, an' tell yer brother Pete ter bring a rope hyar fur me ter climb up by."

Ethan expected to hear the shambling step going away with a celerity proportionate to the importance of the errand. On the contrary, the step was approaching the crag.

A moment of suspense, and there appeared among the jagged ends of the broken vines a small red head, a deeply freckled face, and a pair of sharp, eager blue eyes. George Birt had carefully laid himself down on his stomach, only protruding his head beyond the verge of the crag, that he might not fling away his life in his curiosity.

"Did ye git it?" he asked, with bated breath.

"Git what?" demanded poor Ethan, surprised and impatient.

"The tur-r-key — what ye hev done been talkin' 'bout," said George Birt.

Ethan had lost all interest in the turkey. "Yes, yes; but run along, bub. I mought fall off'n this hyar place, — I 'm gittin' stiff sittin' still so long, — or the wind mought blow me off. The wind is blowin' toler'ble brief."

"Gobbler or hen?" asked George Birt eagerly.

"It air a hen," said Ethan. "But look-a-hyar, George, I 'm a-waitin' on ye, an' ef I 'd fall off'n this hyar place, I 'd be ez dead ez a door-nail in a minute."

"Waal, I 'm goin' now," said George Birt, with gratifying alacrity. He raised himself from his recumbent position, and Ethan heard him shambling off, kicking every now and then at the fallen leaves as he went.

Presently, however, he turned and walked back nearly to the brink of the cliff. Then he prostrated himself once more at full length, — for the mountain children are very careful of the precipices, — snaked along dexterously to the verge of the crag, and protruding his red head cautiously, began to parley once more, trading on Ethan's necessities.

" Ef I go on this yerrand fur ye," he said, looking very sharp indeed, " will ye gimme one o' the whings of that thar wild tur-r-key?"

He coveted the wing-feathers, not the joint of the fowl. The " whing " of the domestic turkey is used by the mountain women as a fan, and is considered an elegance as well as a comfort. George Birt aped the customs of his elders, regardless of sex, — a characteristic of very small boys.

" Oh, go 'long, bubby!" exclaimed poor Ethan, in dismay at the dilatoriness and indifference of his unique deliverer. " I 'll give ye both o' the whings." He would have offered the turkey willingly, if " bubby " had seemed to crave it.

" Waal, I 'm goin' now."

George Birt rose from the ground and started off briskly, exhilarated by the promise of both the " whings."

Ethan was angry indeed when he heard the boy once more shambling back. Of course one should regard a deliverer with gratitude, especially a deliverer from mortal peril; but it may be doubted if Ethan's gratitude would have been great enough to insure that small red head against a vigorous rap, if it had been within rapping distance, when it was once more cautiously protruded over the verge of the cliff.

" I kem back hyar ter tell ye," the doughty deliverer began, with an air of great importance, and magnifying his office with an extreme relish, " that I can't go an' tell Pete 'bout'n the rope till I hev done kem back from the mill. I hev got old Sorrel hitched out hyar a piece, with a bag o' corn on his back, what I hev ter git ground at the mill. My mother air a-settin' at home now a-waitin' fur that thar corn-meal ter bake dodgers with. An' I hev got a dime ter pay at the mill;

it war lent ter my dad las' week.   An' I 'm
afeard ter walk about much with this hyar
dime; I mought lose it, ye know.   An' I
can't go home 'thout the meal; I 'll ketch it
ef I do.   But I 'll tell Pete arter I git back
from the mill."

"The mill!" echoed Ethan, aghast.   "What
air ye doin' on this side o' the mounting, ef
ye air a-goin' ter the mill?   This ain't the
way ter the mill."

"I kem over hyar," said the little boy, still
with much importance of manner, notwith-
standing a slight suggestion of embarrassment
on his freckled face, "ter see 'bout'n a trap
that I hev sot fur squir'ls.   I 'll see 'bout my
trap, an' then I hev ter go ter the mill, 'kase
my mother air a-settin' in our house now
a-waitin' fur meal ter bake corn-dodgers.
Then I 'll tell Pete whar ye air, an' what ye
said 'bout'n the rope.   Ye must jes' wait fur
me hyar."

Poor Ethan could do nothing else.

As the echo of the boy's shambling step
died in the distance, a redoubled sense of

loneliness fell upon Ethan Tynes. But he
endeavored to solace himself with the reflection that the important mission to the squirrel-
trap and the errand to the mill could not last
forever, and before a great while Peter Birt
and his rope would be upon the crag.

This idea buoyed him up as the hours crept
slowly by. Now and then he lifted his head
and listened with painful intentness. He felt
stiff in every muscle, and yet he had a dread
of making an effort to change his constrained
position. He might lose control of his rigid
limbs, and fall into those dread depths beneath.

His patience at last began to give way.
His heart was sinking. His messenger had
been even more dilatory than he was prepared
to expect. Why did not Pete come? Was
it possible that George had forgotten to tell
of his danger?

The sun was going down, leaving a great
glory of gold and crimson clouds and an
opaline haze upon the purple mountains. The
last rays fell on the bronze feathers of the

turkey still lying tied to the broken vines on the ledge.

And now there were only frowning masses of dark clouds in the west; and there were frowning masses of clouds overhead.

The shadow of the coming night had fallen on the autumnal foliage in the deep valley; in the place of the opaline haze was only a gray mist.

And now came, sweeping along between the parallel mountain ranges, a sombre rain-cloud. The lad could hear the heavy drops splashing on the treetops in the valley, long, long before he felt them on his head.

The roll of thunder sounded among the crags. Then the rain came down tumultuously, not in columns, but in livid sheets. The lightnings rent the sky, showing, as it seemed to him, glimpses of the glorious brightness within, — too bright for human eyes.

He clung desperately to his precarious perch. Now and then a fierce rush of wind almost tore him from it. Strange fancies beset him. The air was full of that wild symphony of nature, the wind and the rain, the pealing thunder, and the thunderous echo among the cliffs, and yet he thought he could hear his own name ringing again and again through all the tumult, sometimes in Pete's voice, sometimes in George's shrill tones.

He became vaguely aware, after a time, that the rain had ceased, and the moon was beginning to shine through rifts in the clouds.

The wind continued unabated, but, curiously enough, he could not hear it now. He could hear nothing; he could think of nothing. His consciousness was beginning to fail.

George Birt had indeed forgotten him, — forgotten even the promised " whings." Not that he had discovered anything so extraordinary in his trap, for his trap was empty, but when he reached the mill, he found that the miller had killed a bear and captured a cub, and the orphan, chained to a post, had deeply absorbed George Birt's attention.

To sophisticated people, the boy might have

seemed as grotesque as the cub. George wore
an unbleached cotton shirt. The waistband
of his baggy jeans trousers encircled his
body just beneath his armpits, reaching to
his shoulder-blades behind, and nearly to his
collar-bone in front. His red head was only
partly covered by a fragment of an old white
wool hat; and he looked at the cub with a
curiosity as intense as that with which the
cub looked at him. Each was taking first
lessons in natural history.

As long as there was daylight enough left
to see that cub, did George Birt stand and
stare at the little beast. Then he clattered
home on old Sorrel in the closing darkness,
looking like a very small pin on the top of a
large pincushion.

At home, he found the elders unreasonable,
— as elders usually are considered. Supper
had been waiting an hour or so for the lack
of meal for dodgers. He "caught it" con-
siderably, but not sufficiently to impair his
appetite for the dodgers. After all this, he
was ready enough for bed when small boy's

bedtime came. But as he was nodding before the fire, he heard a word that roused him to a new excitement.

"These hyar chips air so wet they won't burn," said his mother. "I 'll take my tur-r-key whing an' fan the fire."

"Law!" he exclaimed. "Thar, now! Ethan Tynes never gimme that thar wild tur-r-key's whings like he promised."

"Whar did ye happen ter see Ethan?" asked Pete, interested in his friend.

"Seen him in the woods, an' he promised me the tur-r-key whings."

"What fur?" inquired Pete, a little surprised by this uncalled-for generosity.

"Waal," — there was an expression of embarrassment on the important freckled face, and the small red head nodded forward in an explanatory manner, — "he fell off'n the bluffs arter the tur-r-key whings — I mean, he went down to the ledge arter the tur-r-key, and the vines bruk an' he could n't git up no more. An' he tole me that ef I 'd tell ye ter fotch him a rope ter pull up by, he would

gimme the whings.   That happened a — leetle
— while — arter dinner-time."

"Who got him a rope ter pull up by?"
demanded Pete.

There was again on the important face
that indescribable shade of embarrassment.
"Waal," — the youngster balanced this word
judicially, — "I forgot 'bout'n the tur-r-key
whings till this minute.   I reckon he's thar
yit."

"Mebbe this hyar wind an' rain hev beat
him off'n the ledge!" exclaimed Pete, appalled, and rising hastily.   "I tell ye now,"
he added, turning to his mother, "the best
use ye kin make o' that thar boy is ter put
him on the fire fur a back-log."

Pete made his preparations in great haste.
He took the rope from the well, asked the
crestfallen and browbeaten junior a question
or two relative to locality, mounted old Sorrel without a saddle, and in a few minutes
was galloping at headlong speed through the
night.

The rain was over by the time he had

reached the sulphur spring to which George had directed him, but the wind was still high, and the broken clouds were driving fast across the face of the moon.

When he had hitched his horse to a tree, and set out on foot to find the cliff, the moonbeams, though brilliant, were so intermittent that his progress was fitful and necessarily cautious. When the disk shone out full and clear, he made his way rapidly enough, but when the clouds intervened, he stood still and waited.

"I ain't goin' ter fall off'n the bluff 'thout knowin' it," he said to himself, in one of these eclipses, "ef I hev ter stand hyar all night."

The moonlight was brilliant and steady when he reached the verge of the crag. He identified the spot by the mass of broken vines, and more indubitably by Ethan's rifle lying upon the ground just at his feet. He called, but received no response.

"Hev Ethan fell off, sure enough?" he asked himself, in great dismay and alarm. Then he shouted again and again. At last there came an answer, as though the speaker had just awaked.

"Pretty nigh beat out, I 'm a-thinkin' !" commented Pete. He tied one end of the cord around the trunk of a tree, knotted it at intervals, and flung it over the bluff.

At first Ethan was almost afraid to stir. He slowly put forth his hand and grasped the rope. Then, his heart beating tumultuously, he rose to his feet.

He stood still for an instant to steady himself and get his breath. Nerving himself for a strong effort, he began the ascent, hand over hand, up, and up, and up, till once more he stood upon the crest of the crag.

And, now that all danger was over, Pete was disposed to scold. "I 'm a-thinkin'," said Pete severely, "ez thar ain't a critter on this hyar mounting, from a b'ar ter a copperhead, that could hev got in sech a fix, 'ceptin' ye, Ethan Tynes."

And Ethan was silent.

"What 's this hyar thing at the e-end o' the rope?" asked Pete, as he began to draw the cord up, and felt a weight still suspended.

" It air the tur-r-key," said Ethan meekly. "I tied her ter the e-end o' the rope afore I kem up."

" Waal, sir ! " exclaimed Pete, in indignant surprise.

And George, for duty performed, was remunerated with the two " whings," although it still remains a question in the mind of Ethan whether or not he deserved them.

IN THE "CHINKING"

Not far from an abrupt precipice on a certain great mountain spur there stands in the midst of the red and yellow autumn woods a little log "church-house." The nuts rattle noisily down on its roof; sometimes during "evenin' preachin'" — which takes place in the afternoon — a flying-squirrel frisks near the window; the hymns echo softly, softly, from the hazy sunlit heights across the valley.

"That air the doxol'gy," said Tom Brent, one day, pausing to listen among the wagons and horses hitched outside. He was about to follow home his father's mare, that had broken loose and galloped off through the woods, but as he glanced back at the church, a sudden thought struck him. He caught sight of the end of little Jim Coggin's comforter flaunting out through the "chinking,"

— as the mountaineers call the series of short slats which are set diagonally in the spaces between the logs of the walls, and on which the clay is thickly daubed. This work had been badly done, and in many places the daubing had fallen away. Thus it was that as Jim Coggin sat within the church, the end of his plaid comforter had slipped through the chinking and was waving in the wind outside.

Now Jim had found the weather still too warm for his heavy jeans jacket, but he was too cool without it, and he had ingeniously compromised the difficulty by wearing his comforter in this unique manner, — laying it on his shoulders, crossing it over the chest, passing it under the arms, and tying it in a knot between the shoulder-blades. Tom remembered this with a grin as he slyly crept up to the house, and it was only the work of a moment to draw that knot through the chinking and secure it firmly to a sumach bush that grew near at hand.

It never occurred to him that the resound-

ing doxology could fail to rouse that small,
tow-headed, freckle-faced boy, or that the
congregation might slowly disperse without
noticing him as he sat motionless and asleep
in the dark shadow.

The sun slipped down into the red west;
the blue mountains turned purple; heavy
clouds gathered, and within three miles there
was no other human creature when Jim suddenly woke to the darkness and the storm
and the terrible loneliness.

Where was he? He tried to rise: he
could not move. Bewildered, he struggled
and tugged at his harness, — all in vain. As
he realized the situation, he burst into tears.

" Them home-folks o' mine won't kem hyar
ter s'arch fur me," he cried desperately, " kase
I tole my mother ez how I war a-goin' ter dust
down the mounting ter Aunt Jerushy's house
ez soon ez meet'n' war out an' stay all night
along o' her boys."

Still he tried to comfort himself by reflect-
ing that it was not so bad as it might have
been. There was no danger that he would

have to starve and pine here till next Sunday, for a "protracted meeting" was in progress, service was held every day, and the congregation would return to-morrow, which was Thursday.

His philosophy, however, was short-lived, for the sudden lightning rent the clouds, and a terrific peal of thunder echoed among the cliffs.

"The storm air a-comin' up the mounting!" he exclaimed, in vivacious protest. "An' ef this brief wind war ter whurl the old church-house off'n the bluff an' down inter the valley whar-r — would — I — be?"

All at once the porch creaked beneath a heavy tread. A clumsy hand was fumbling at the door. "Strike a light," said a gruff voice without.

As a lantern was thrust in, Jim was about to speak, but the words froze upon his lips for fear when a man strode heavily over the threshold and he caught the expression of his face.

It was an evil face, red and bloated and

brutish. He had small, malicious, twinkling eyes, and a shock of sandy hair. A suit of copper-colored jeans hung loosely on his tall, lank frame, and when he placed the lantern on a bench and stretched out both arms as if he were tired, he showed that his left hand was maimed, — the thumb had been cut off at the first joint.

A thickset, short, swaggering man tramped in after him.

" Waal, Amos Brierwood," he said, " it 's safes' fur us ter part. We oughter be fur enough from hyar by daybreak. Divide that thar traveler's money — hey ? "

They carefully closed the rude shutters, barred the door, and sat down on the " mourners' bench," neither having noticed the small boy at the other end of the room.

Poor Jim, his arms akimbo and half-covered by his comforter, stuck to the wall like a plaid bat, — if such a natural curiosity is imaginable, — feverishly hoping that the men might go without seeing him at all.

For surely no human creature could be

more abhorrent, more incredibly odious of aspect, than Amos Brierwood as he sat there, his red, brutish face redder still with a malign pleasure, his malicious eyes gloating over the rolls of money which he drew from a pocket-book stolen from some waylaid traveler, snapping his fingers in exultation when the amount of the bills exceeded his expectation.

The leaves without were fitfully astir, and once the porch creaked suddenly. Brierwood glanced at the door sharply, — even fearfully, — his hand motionless on the rolls of money.

"Only the wind, Amos, only the wind!" said the short, stout man impatiently.

But he, himself, was disquieted the next moment when a horse neighed shrilly.

"That ain't my beastis, Amos, nor yit your'n!" he cried, starting up.

"It air the traveler's, ye sodden idjit!" said Brierwood, lifting his uncouth foot and giving him a jocose kick.

But the short man was not satisfied. He rose, went outside, and Jim could hear him

beating about among the bushes. Presently
he came in again. " 'T war the traveler's
critter, I reckon; an' that critter an' saddle
oughter be counted in my sheer."

Then they fell to disputing and quarreling,
— once they almost fought, — but at length
the division was made and they rose to go.
As Brierwood swung his lantern round, his
malicious eyes fell upon the poor little plaid
bat sticking against the wall.

He stood in the door staring, dumfounded
for a moment. Then he clenched his fist,
and shook it fiercely. " How did ye happen
ter be hyar this time o' the night, ye limb o'
Satan ? " he cried.

" Dunno," faltered poor Jim.

The other man had returned too. " Waal,
sir, ef that thar boy hed been a copper-head
now, he 'd hev bit us, sure ! "

" *He mought do that yit,*" said Amos Brierwood, with grim significance. " He hev been
thar all this time, — 'kase he air tied thar,
don't ye see ? An' he hev *eyes*, an' he hev
ears. What air ter hender ? "

The other man's face turned pale, and Jim thought that they were afraid he would tell all he had seen and heard. The manner of both had changed, too. They had a skulking, nervous way with them now in place of the coarse bravado that had characterized them hitherto.

Amos Brierwood pondered for a few minutes. Then he sullenly demanded, —

" What's yer name ? "

" It air Jeemes Coggin," quavered the little boy.

" Coggin, hey ? " exclaimed Brierwood, with a new idea bringing back the malicious twinkle to his eyes. He laughed as though mightily relieved, and threw up his left hand and shook it exultingly.

The shadow on the dark wall of that maimed hand with only the stump of a thumb was a weird, a horrible thing to the child. He had no idea that his constant notice of it would stamp it in his memory, and that something would come of this fact. He was glad when the shadow ceased to writhe and twist upon the wall, and the man dropped his arm to his side again.

"What's a-brewin', Amos?" asked the other, who had been watching Brierwood curiously.

They whispered aside for a few moments, at first anxiously and then with wild guffaws of satisfaction. When they approached the boy, their manner had changed once more.

"Waal, I declar, bubby," said Brierwood agreeably, "this hyar fix ez ye hev got inter air sateful fur true! It air enough ter sot enny boy on the mounting cat-a-wampus. 'T war a good thing ez we-uns happened ter kem by hyar on our way from the tan-yard way down yander in the valley whar we-uns hev been ter git paid up fur workin' thar some. We'll let ye out. Who done yer this hyar trick?"

"Dunno — witches, I reckon!" cried poor Jim, bursting into tears.

"Witches!" the man exclaimed, "the woods air a-roamin' with 'em this time o' the year; bein', ye see, ez they kem ter feed on the mast."

He chuckled as he said this, perhaps at the boy's evident terror, — for Jim was sorrowfully superstitious, — perhaps because he had managed to cut unnoticed a large fragment from the end of the comforter. This he stuffed into his own pocket as he talked on about two witches, whom he said he had met that afternoon under an oak-tree feeding on acorns.

"An' now, I kem ter remind myself that them witches war inquirin' round 'bout'n a boy — war his name Jeemes Coggin? Le''s see! That boy's name *war* Jeemes Coggin!"

While Jim stood breathlessly, intently listening, Brierwood had twisted something into the folds of his comforter so dexterously that unless this were untied it would not fall; it was a silk handkerchief of a style never before seen in the mountains, and he had made a knot hard and fast in one corner.

"Thar, now!" he exclaimed, holding up the fragment of knitted yarn, "I hev tore yer comforter. Never mind, bubby, 't war tore afore. But it 'll do ter wrop up this

money-purse what b'longs ter yer dad. He
lef' it hid in the chinking o' the wall over
yander close ter whar I war sittin' when I fust
kem in.   I 'll put it back thar, 'kase yer dad
don't want nobody ter know whar it air hid."

He strode across the room and concealed
the empty pocket-book in the chinking.

" Ef ye won't tell who teched it, I 'll gin a
good word fur ye ter them witches what war
inquirin' round fur ye ter-day."

Jim promised in hot haste, and then, the
rain having ceased, he started for home, but
Brierwood stopped him at the door.

" Hold on thar, bub.   I kem mighty nigh
furgittin' ter let ye know ez I seen yer brother Alf awhile back, an' he axed me ter git
ye ter go by Tom Brent's house, an' tell Tom
ter meet him up the road a piece by that thar
big sulphur spring. Will ye gin Tom that
message? Tell him Alf said ter come quick."

Once more Jim promised.

The two men holding the lantern out in the
porch watched him as he pounded down the
dark road, his tow hair sticking out of his

tattered black hat, the ends of his comforter flaunting in the breeze, and every gesture showing the agitated haste of a witch-scared boy. Then they looked at each other significantly, and laughed loud and long.

" He 'll tell sech a crooked tale ter-morrer that Alf Coggin an' his dad will see sights along o' that traveler's money!" said Brier-wood, gloating over his sharp management as he and his accomplice mounted their horses and rode off in opposite directions.

When Jim reached Tom Brent's house, and knocked at the door, he was so absorbed in his terrors that, as it opened, he said nothing for a moment. He could see the family group within. Tom's father was placidly smoking. His palsied " gran'dad " shook in his chair in the chimney-corner as he told the wide-eyed boys big tales about the " Injuns " that harried the early settlers in Tennessee.

" Tom," Jim said, glancing up at the big boy, — " Tom, thar 's a witch waitin' fur ye at the sulphur spring! Go thar, quick!"

" Not ef I knows what 's good fur me !"

protested Tom, with a great horse-laugh. "What ails ye, boy? Ye talk like ye war teched in the head!"

"I went ter say ez Alf Coggin air thar waitin' fur ye," Jim began again, nodding his slandered head with great solemnity, "an' tole me ter tell ye ter kem thar quick."

He took no heed of the inaccuracy of the message; he was glancing fearfully over his shoulder, and the next minute scuttled down the road in a bee-line for home.

Tom hurried off briskly through the woods. "Waal, sir! I'm mighty nigh crazed ter know what Alf Coggin kin want o' me; goin' coon-huntin', mebbe," he speculated, as he drew within sight of an old lightning-scathed tree which stood beside the sulphur spring and stretched up, stark and white, in the dim light.

The clouds were blowing away from a densely instarred sky; the moon was hardly more than a crescent and dipping low in the west, but he could see the sombre outline of the opposite mountain, and the white mists that shifted in a ghostly and elusive fashion along the summit. The night was still, save for a late katydid, spared by the frost, and piping shrilly.

He experienced a terrible shock of surprise when a sudden voice — a voice he had never heard before — cried out sharply, "Hello there! Help! help!"

As he pressed tremulously forward, he beheld a sight which made him ask himself if it were possible that Alf Coggin had sent for him to join in some nefarious work which had ended in leaving a man — a stranger — bound to the old lightning-scathed tree.

Even in the uncertain light Tom could see that he was pallid and panting, evidently exhausted in some desperate struggle : there was blood on his face, his clothes were torn, and by all odds he was the angriest man that was ever waylaid and robbed.

"Ter-morrer he 'll be jes' a-swoopin' !" thought Tom, tremulously untying the complicated knots, and listening to his threats of vengeance on the unknown robbers, "an' every critter on the mounting will git a clutch from his claws."

And in fact, it was hardly daybreak before the constable of the district, who lived hard by in the valley, was informed of all the details of the affair, so far as known to Tom or the " Traveler," — for thus the mountaineers designated him, as if he were the only one in the world.

By reason of the message which Jim had delivered, and its strange result, they suspected the Coggins, and as they rode together to the justice's house for a warrant, this suspicion received unexpected confirmation in a rumor that they found afloat. Every man they met stopped them to repeat the story that Coggin's boy had told somebody that it was his father who had robbed the traveler, and hid the empty pocket-book in the chinking of the church wall. No one knew who had set this report in circulation, but a blacksmith said he heard it first from a man named Brierwood, who had stopped at his shop to have his horse shod.

It was still early when they reached Jim Coggin's home; the windows and doors were open to let out the dust, for his mother was just beginning to sweep. She had pushed aside the table, when her eyes suddenly distended with surprise as they fell upon a silk handkerchief lying on the floor beside it. The moment that she stooped and picked it up, the strange gentleman stepped upon the porch, and through the open door he saw it dangling from her hands.

He tapped the constable on the shoulder.

"That's my property!" he said tersely.

The officer stepped in instantly. "Good-mornin', Mrs. Coggin," he said politely. "'T would pleasure me some ter git a glimpse o' that handkercher."

" Air it your'n ? " asked the woman wonderingly. " I jes' now fund it, an' I war tried ter know who had drapped it hyar."

The officer, without a word, untied the knot which Amos Brierwood had made in one corner, while the Coggins looked on in open-mouthed amazement. It contained a five-dollar bill, and a bit of paper on which some careless memoranda had been jotted down in handwriting which the traveler claimed as his own.

It seemed a very plain case. Still, he got out of the sound of the woman's sobs and cries as soon as he conveniently could, and sauntered down the road, where the officer presently overtook him with Alf and his father in custody.

" Whar be ye a-takin' of us now ? " cried the elder, gaunt and haggard, and with his long hair blowing in the breeze.

" Ter the church-house, whar yer boy says ye hev hid the traveler's money-purse," said the officer.

" *My boy !* " exclaimed John Coggin, casting an astounded glance upon his son.

Poor Alf was almost stunned. When they reached the church, and the men, after searching for a time without result, appealed to him to save trouble by pointing out the spot where the pocket-book was concealed, he could only stammer and falter unintelligibly, and finally he burst into tears.

" Ax the t'other one — the leetle boy,"
suggested an old man in the crowd.

Alf's heart sank — sank like lead — when
Jim, suddenly remembering the promised
"good word" to the witches, piped out, " I
war tole not ter tell who teched it, — 'kase
my dad did n't want nobody ter know 't war
hid thar."

John Coggin's face was rigid and gray.

" The Lord hev forsook me ! " he cried.
" An' all my chillen hev turned liars tergether."

Then he made a great effort to control
himself.

" Look-a-hyar, Jim, ef ye hev got the truth
in ye, — speak it !   Ef ye know whar I hev
hid anything, — find it ! "

Jim, infinitely important, and really under-
standing little of what was going on, except
that all these big men were looking at him,
crossed the room with as much stateliness as
is compatible with a pair of baggy brown
jeans trousers, a plaid comforter tied between
the shoulder-blades in a big knot, a tow-head,

and a tattered black hat; he slipped his grimy paw in the chinking where Amos Brierwood had hid the pocket-book, and drew it thence, with the prideful exclamation, —

" B'longs ter my dad ! "

The officer held it up empty before the traveler, — he held up, too, the bit of comforter in which it was folded, and pointed to the small boy's shoulders. The gentleman turned away, thoroughly convinced. Alf and his father looked from one to the other, in mute despair. They foresaw many years of imprisonment for a crime which they had not committed.

The constable was hurrying his prisoners toward the door, when there was a sudden stir on the outskirts of the crowd. Old Parson Payne was pushing his way in, followed by a tall young man, who, in comparison with the mountaineers, seemed wonderfully prosperous and well-clad, and very fresh and breezy.

" You 're all on the wrong track ! " he cried.

And his story proved this, though it was simple enough.

He was sojourning in the mountains with some friends on a "camp-hunt," and the previous evening he had chanced to lose his way in the woods. When night and the storm came on, he was perhaps five miles from camp. He mistook the little "church-house" for a dwelling, and dismounting, he hitched his horse in the laurel, intending to ask for shelter for the night. As he stepped upon the porch, however, he caught a glimpse, through the chinking, of the interior, and he perceived that the building was a church. There were benches and a rude pulpit. The next instant, his attention was riveted by the sight of two men, one of whom had drawn a knife upon the other, quarreling over a roll of money. He stood rooted to the spot in surprise. Gradually, he began to understand the villainy afoot, for he overheard all that they said to each other, and afterward to Jim. He saw one of the men cut the bit from the comforter, wrap the pocket-book in it, and hide it away, and he witnessed a dispute between them, which went on in dumb show behind the boy's back, as to which of two bills should be knotted in the handkerchief which they twisted into the comforter.

The constable was pressing him to describe the appearance of the ruffians.

"Why," said the stranger, "one of them was long, and lank, and loose-jointed, and had sandy hair, and " — He paused abruptly, cudgeling his memory for something more distinctive, for this description would apply to half the men in the room, and thus it would be impossible to identify and capture the robbers.

"He hed n't no thumb sca'cely on his lef' hand," piped out Jim, holding up his own grimy paw, and looking at it with squinting intensity as he crooked it at the first joint, to imitate the maimed hand.

"No thumb!" exclaimed the constable excitedly. "Amos Brierwood fur a thousand!"

Jim nodded his head intelligently, with sudden recollection. "That air the name ez the chunky man gin him when they fust kem in."

And thus it was that when the Coggins were presently brought before the justice, they were exonerated of all complicity in the crime for which Brierwood and his accomplice were afterward arrested, tried, and sentenced to the State Prison.

Jim doubts whether the promised "good word" was ever spoken on his behalf to the witches, who were represented as making personal inquiries about him, because he suspects that the two robbers were themselves the only evil spirits roaming the woods that night.

ON A HIGHER LEVEL

As Jack Dunn stood in the door of his home on a great crag of Persimmon Ridge and loaded his old rifle, his eyes rested upon a vast and imposing array of mountains filling the landscape. All are heavily wooded, all are alike, save that in one the long horizontal line of the summit is broken by a sudden vertical ascent, and thence the mountain seems to take up life on a higher level, for it sinks no more and passes out of sight.

This abrupt rise is called "Elijah's Step," — named, perhaps, in honor of some neighboring farmer who first explored it; but the ignorant boy believed that here the prophet had stepped into his waiting fiery chariot.

He knew of no foreign lands, — no Syria, no Palestine. He had no dream of the world that lay beyond those misty, azure hills. Indistinctly he had caught the old story from the nasal drawl of the circuit-rider, and he thought that here, among these wild Tennessee mountains, Elijah had lived and had not died.

There came suddenly from the valley the baying of a pack of hounds in full cry, and when the crags caught the sound and tossed it from mountain to mountain, when more delicate echoes on a higher key rang out from the deep ravines, there was a wonderful exhilaration in this sylvan minstrelsy. The young fellow looked wistful as he heard it, then he frowned heavily.

"Them thar Saunders men hev gone off an' left me," he said reproachfully to some one within the log cabin. "Hyar I be kept a-choppin' wood an' a pullin' fodder till they hev hed time ter git up a deer. It 'pears ter me ez I mought hev been let ter put off that thar work till I war through huntin'."

He was a tall young fellow, with a frank, freckled face and auburn hair; stalwart, too. Judging from his appearance, he could chop wood and pull fodder to some purpose.

A heavy, middle-aged man emerged from the house, and stood regarding his son with grim disfavor. "An' who oughter chop wood an' pull fodder but ye, while my hand air sprained this way?" he demanded.

That hand had been sprained for many a long day, but the boy made no reply; perhaps he knew its weight. He walked to the verge of the cliff, and gazed down at the tops of the trees in the valley far, far below.

The expanse of foliage was surging in the wind like the waves of the sea. From the unseen depths beneath there rose again the cry of the pack, inexpressibly stirring, and replete with woodland suggestions. All the echoes came out to meet it.

"I war promised ter go!" cried Jack bitterly.

"Waal," said his mother, from within the house, "'t ain't no good nohow."

Her voice was calculated to throw oil upon the troubled waters, — low, languid, and full of pacifying intonations. She was a tall, thin woman, clad in a blue-checked homespun dress,

and seated before a great hand-loom, as a lady
sits before a piano or an organ. The creak
of the treadle, and the thump, thump of the
batten, punctuated, as it were, her consolatory
disquisition.

Her son looked at her in great depression
of spirit as she threw the shuttle back and
forth with deft, practiced hands.

"Wild meat air a mighty savin'," she continued, with a housewifely afterthought. "I
ain't denyin' that."

Thump, thump, went the batten.

"But ye need n't pester the life out'n yerself 'kase ye ain't a-runnin' the deer along o'
them Saunders men. It 'pears like a powerful
waste o' time, when ye kin take yer gun down
ter the river enny evenin' late, jes' ez the deer
air goin' ter drink, an' shoot ez big a buck
ez ye hev got the grit ter git enny other way.
Ye can't do nothin' with a buck but eat him,
an' a-runnin' him all around the mounting
don't make him no tenderer, ter my mind. I
don't see no sense in huntin' 'cept ter git
somethin' fitten ter eat."

This logic, enough to break a sportsman's heart, was not a panacea for the tedium of the day, spent in the tame occupation of pulling fodder, as the process of stripping the blades from the standing cornstalks is called.

But when the shadows were growing long, Jack took his rifle and set out for the profit and the pleasure of still-hunting. As he made his way through the dense woods, the metallic tones of a cow-bell jangled on the air, — melodious sound in the forest quiet, but it conjured up a scowl on the face of the young mountaineer.

" Everything on this hyar mounting hev got the twistin's ter-day ! " he exclaimed wrathfully. " Hyar is our old red cow a-traipsing off ter Andy Bailey's house, an' thar won't be a drap of milk for supper."

This was a serious matter, for in a region where coffee and tea are almost unknown luxuries, and the evening meal consists of such thirst-provoking articles as broiled venison, corn-dodgers, and sorghum, one is apt to feel the need of some liquid milder than

" apple-jack," and more toothsome than water, wherewith to wet one's whistle.

In common with everything else on the mountain, Jack, too, had the "twistin's," and it was with a sour face that he began to drive the cow homeward. After going some distance, however, he persuaded himself that she would leave the beaten track no more until she reached the cabin. He turned about, therefore, and retraced his way to the stream.

There had been heavy rains in the mountains, and it was far out of its banks, rushing and foaming over great rocks, circling in swift whirlpools, plunging in smooth, glassy sheets down sudden descents, and maddening thence in tumultuous, yeasty billows.

An old mill, long disused and fallen into decay, stood upon the brink. It was a painful suggestion of collapsed energies, despite its picturesque drapery of vines. No human being could live there, but in the doorway abruptly appeared a boy of seventeen, dressed, like Jack, in an old brown jeans suit and a shapeless white hat.

Jack paused at a little distance up on the hill, and parleyed in a stentorian voice with the boy in the mill.

"What's the reason ye air always tryin' ter toll off our old red muley from our house?" he demanded angrily.

"I ain't never tried ter toll her off," said Andy Bailey. "She jes' kem ter our house herself. I dunno ez I hev got enny call ter look arter other folkses' stray cattle. Mind yer own cow."

"I hev got a mighty notion ter cut down that thar sapling," — and Jack pointed to a good-sized hickory-tree, — "an' wear it out on ye."

"I ain't afeard. Come on!" said Andy impudently, protected by his innocence, and the fact of being the smaller of the two.

There was a pause. "Hev ye been a-huntin'?" asked Jack, beginning to be mollified by the rare luxury of youthful and congenial companionship; for this was a scantily settled region, and boys were few.

Andy nodded assent.

Jack walked down into the rickety mill, and stood leaning against the rotten old hopper. " What did ye git ? " he said, looking about for the game.

" Waal," drawled Andy, with much hesitation, " I hain't been started out long." He turned from the door and faced his companion rather sheepishly.

" I hopes ye ain't been poppin' off that rifle o' your'n along that deer-path down in the hollow, an' a-skeerin' off all the wild critters," said Jack Dunn, with sudden apprehension. " Ef I war ez pore a shot ez ye air, I'd go a-huntin' with a bean-pole instead of a gun, an' leave the game ter them that kin shoot it."

Andy was of a mercurial and nervous temperament, and this fact perhaps may account for the anomaly of a mountain-boy who was a poor shot. Andy was the scoff of Persimmon Ridge.

" I hev seen many a gal who could shoot ez well ez ye kin, — better," continued Jack jeeringly. " But law ! I need n't kerry my

heavy bones down thar in the hollow expectin'
ter git a deer ter-day. They air all off in
the woods a-smellin' the powder ye hev been
wastin'."

Andy was pleased to change the subject.
" It 'pears ter me that that thar water air
a-scuttlin' along toler'ble fast," he said, turning his eyes to the little window through
which the stream could be seen.

It *was* running fast, and with a tremendous
force. One could obtain some idea of the
speed and impetus of the current from the
swift vehemence with which logs and branches
shot past, half hidden in foam.

The water looked black with this white contrast. Here and there a great, grim rock
projected sharply above the surface. In the
normal condition of the stream, these were its
overhanging banks, but now, submerged, they
gave to its flow the character of rapids.

The old mill, its wooden supports submerged
too, trembled and throbbed with the throb-
bing water. As Jack looked toward the window, his eyes were suddenly distended, his

cheek paled, and he sprang to the door with a frightened exclamation.

Too late! the immense bole of a fallen tree, shooting down the channel with the force and velocity of a great projectile, struck the tottering supports of the crazy, rotting building.

It careened, and quivered in every fibre; there was a crash of falling timbers, then a mighty wrench, and the two boys, clinging to the window-frame, were driving with the wreck down the river.

The old mill thundered against the submerged rocks, and at every concussion the timbers fell. It whirled around and around in eddying pools. Where the water was clear, and smooth, and deep, it shot along with great rapidity.

The convulsively clinging boys looked down upon the black current, with its sharp, treacherous, half-seen rocks and ponderous driftwood. The wild idea of plunging into the tumult and trying to swim to the bank faded as they looked. Here in the crazy building there might be a chance. In that frightful swirl there lurked only a grim certainty.

The house had swung along in the middle of the stream; now its course was veering slightly to the left. This could be seen through the window and the interstices of the half-fallen timbers.

The boys were caged, as it were; the doorway was filled with the heavy debris, and the only possibility of escape was through that little window. It was so small that only one could pass through at a time, — only one could be saved.

Jack had seen the chance from far up the stream. There was a stretch of smooth water close in to the bank, on which was a low-hanging beech-tree, — he might catch the branches.

They were approaching the spot with great rapidity. Only one could go. He himself had discovered the opportunity, — it was his own.

Life was sweet, — so sweet! He could not give it up; he could not now take thought for his friend. He could only hope with a frenzied eagerness that Andy had not seen the possibility of deliverance.

In another moment Andy lifted himself into the window. A whirlpool caught the wreck, and there it eddied in dizzying circles. It was not yet too late. Jack could tear the smaller, weaker fellow away with one strong hand, and take the only chance for escape. The shattered mill was dashing through the smoother waters now; the great beech-tree was hanging over their heads; an inexplicable, overpowering impulse mastered in an instant Jack's temptation.

"Ketch the branches, Andy!" he cried wildly.

His friend was gone, and he was whirling off alone on those cruel, frantic waters. In the midst of the torrent he was going down, and down, and down the mountain.

Now and then he had a fleeting glimpse of the distant ranges. There was "Elijah's Step," glorified in the sunset, purple and splendid, with red and gold clouds flaming above it. To his untutored imagination they looked like the fiery chariot again awaiting the prophet.

The familiar sight, the familiar, oft-repeated fancy, the recollection of his home, brought sudden tears to his eyes. He gazed wistfully at the spot whence he believed the man had ascended who left death untasted, and then he went on in this mad rush down to the bitterness of death.

Even with this terrible fact before him, he did not reproach himself with his costly generosity. It was strange to him that he did not regret it; perhaps, like that mountain, he had suddenly taken up life on a higher level.

The sunset splendor was fading. The fiery chariot was gone, and in its place were floating gray clouds, — the dust of its wheels, they seemed. The outlines of " Elijah's Step " were dark. It looked sad, bereaved. Its glory had departed.

Suddenly the whole landscape seemed full of reeling black shadows, — and yet it was

IN THE MIDST OF THE TORRENT

not night. The roar of the torrent was growing faint upon his ear, and yet its momentum was unchecked. Soon all was dark and all was still, and the world slipped from his grasp.

"They tell me that thar Jack Dunn war mighty nigh drownded when them men fished him out'n the pond at Skeggs's sawmill down thar in the valley," said Andy Bailey, recounting the incident to the fireside circle at his own home. "They seen them rotten old timbers come a-floatin' ez peaceable on to the pond, an' then they seen somethin' like a human a-hangin' ter 'em. The water air ez still ez a floor thar, an' deep an' smooth, an' they did n't hev no trouble in swimmin' out to him. They could n't bring him to, though, at fust. They said in a little more he would hev been gone sure! Now" — pridefully — "ef he hed hed the grit ter ketch a tree an' pull out, like I done, he would n't hev been in sech a danger."

Andy never knew the sacrifice his friend had made. Jack never told him. Applause is at best a slight thing. A great action is nobler than the monument that commemorates it ; and when a man gives himself into the control of a generous impulse, thenceforward he takes up life on a higher level.

CHRISTMAS DAY ON OLD WINDY MOUNTAIN

THE sun had barely shown the rim of his great red disk above the sombre woods and snow-crowned crags of the opposite ridge, when Rick Herne, his rifle in his hand, stepped out of his father's log cabin, perched high among the precipices of Old Windy Mountain. He waited motionless for a moment, and all the family trooped to the door to assist at the time-honored ceremony of firing a salute to the day.

Suddenly the whole landscape catches a rosy glow, Rick whips up his rifle, a jet of flame darts swiftly out, a sharp report rings all around the world, and the sun goes grandly up — while the little tow-headed mountaineers hurrah shrilly for " Chris'mus ! "

As he began to re-load his gun, the small boys clustered around him, their hands in the pockets of their baggy jeans trousers, their heads inquiringly askew.

"They air a-goin' ter hev a pea-fow*el* fur dinner down yander ter Birk's Mill," Rick remarked.

The smallest boy smacked his lips, — not that he knew how pea-fowl tastes, but he imagined unutterable things.

"Somehows I hates fur ye ter go ter eat at Birk's Mill, they air sech a set o' drinkin' men down thar ter Malviny's house," said Rick's mother, as she stood in the doorway, and looked anxiously at him.

For his elder sister was Birk's wife, and to this great feast he was invited as a representative of the family, his father being disabled by "rheumatics," and his mother kept at home by the necessity of providing dinner for those four small boys.

"Hain't I done promised ye not ter tech a drap o' liquor this Chris'mus day?" asked Rick.

"That's a fac'," his mother admitted. "But boys, an' men-folks ginerally, air scandalous easy ter break a promise whar whiskey is in it."

"I'll hev ye ter know that when I gin my word, I keeps it!" cried Rick pridefully.

He little dreamed how that promise was to be assailed before the sun should go down.

He was a tall, sinewy boy, deft of foot as all these mountaineers are, and a seven-mile walk in the snow to Birk's Mill he considered a mere trifle. He tramped along cheerily enough through the silent solitudes of the dense forest. Only at long intervals the stillness was broken by the cracking of a bough under the weight of snow, or the whistling of a gust of wind through the narrow valley far below.

All at once — it was a terrible shock of surprise — he was sinking! Was there nothing beneath his feet but the vague depths of air to the base of the mountain? He realized with a quiver of dismay that he had mistaken a huge drift-filled fissure, between a jutting crag and the wall of the ridge, for the solid, snow-covered ground. He tossed his arms about wildly in his effort to grasp something firm. The motion only dislodged the drift. He felt that it was falling, and he was going down — down — down with it. He saw the trees on the summit of Old Windy disappear. He caught one glimpse of the neighboring ridges. Then he was blinded and enveloped in this cruel whiteness. He had a wild idea that he had been delivered to it forever; even in the first thaw it would curl up into a wreath of vapor, and rise from the mountain's side, and take him soaring with it — whither? How they would search these bleak wintry fastnesses for him, — while he was gone sailing with the mist! What would they say at home and at Birk's Mill? One last thought of the " pea-fow*el*," and he seemed to slide swiftly away from the world with the snow.

He was unconscious probably only for a few minutes. When he came to himself, he found that he was lying, half-submerged in the great drift, on the slope of the mountain, and the dark, icicle-begirt cliff towered high above. He stretched his limbs — no bones broken! He could hardly believe that he had fallen unhurt from those heights. He did not appreciate how gradually the snow had slidden down. Being so densely packed, too, it had buoyed him up, and kept him from dashing against the sharp, jagged edges of the rock. He had lost consciousness in the jar when the moving mass was abruptly arrested by a transverse elevation of the ground. He was still a little dizzy and faint, but otherwise uninjured.

Now a great perplexity took hold on him. How was he to make his way back up the mountain, he asked himself, as he looked at the inaccessible cliffs looming high into the air. All the world around him was unfamiliar. Even his wide wanderings had never brought him into this vast, snowy, trackless wilderness, that stretched out on every side. He would be half the day in finding the valley road that led to Birk's Mill. He rose to his feet, and gazed about him in painful indecision. The next moment a thrill shot through him, to which he was unaccustomed. He had never before shaken except with the cold, — but this was fear.

For he heard voices! Not from the cliffs above, — but from below! Not from the dense growth of young pines on the slope of the mountain, — but from the depths of the earth beneath! He stood motionless, listening intently, his eyes distended, and his heart beating fast.

All silence! Not even the wind stirred in the pine thicket. The snow lay heavy among the dark green branches, and every slender needle was encased in ice. Rick rubbed his eyes. It was no dream. There was the thicket; but whose were the voices that had rung out faintly from beneath it?

A crowd of superstitions surged upon him. He cast an affrighted glance at the ghastly snow-covered woods and sheeted earth. He was remembering fireside legends, horrible enough to raise the hair on a sophisticated, educated boy's head; much more horrible, then, to a young backwoodsman like Rick.

On this, the most benign day that ever dawns upon the world, was he led into these endless wastes of forest to be terrified by the " harnts " ?

Suddenly those voices from the earth again ! One was singing a drunken catch, — it broke into falsetto, and ended with an unmistakable hiccup.

Rick's blood came back with a rush.

" I hev never hearn tell o' the hoobies gittin' boozy ! " he said with a laugh. " That 's whar they hev got the upper-hand o' humans."

As he gazed again at the thicket, he saw now something that he had been too much agitated to observe before, — a column of dense smoke that rose from far down the declivity, and seemed to make haste to hide itself among the low-hanging boughs of a clump of fir-trees.

" It 's somebody's house down thar," was Rick's conclusion. " I kin find out the way to Birk's Mill from the folkses."

When he neared the smoke, he paused abruptly, staring once more.

There was no house! The smoke rose from among low pine bushes. Above were the snow-laden branches of the fir.

" Ef thar war a house hyar, I reckon I could see it!" said Rick doubtfully, infinitely mystified.

There was a continual drip, drip of moisture all around. Yet a thaw had not set in. Rick looked up at the gigantic icicles that hung to the crags and glittered in the sun, — not a drop trickled from them. But this fir-tree was dripping, dripping, and the snow had melted away from the nearest pine bushes that clustered about the smoke. There was heat below certainly, a strong heat, and somebody was keeping the fire up steadily.

" An' air it folkses ez live underground like foxes an' sech!" Rick exclaimed, astonished, as he came upon a large, irregularly shaped rift in the rocks, and heard the same reeling voice from within, beginning to sing once more. But for this bacchanalian melody, the noise of Rick's entrance might have given notice of his approach. As it was, the inhabitants of this strange place were even more surprised than he, when, after groping through a dark, low passage, an abrupt turn brought him into a lofty, vaulted subterranean apartment. There was a great flare of light, which revealed six or seven muscular men grouped about a large copper vessel built into a rude stone furnace, and all the air was pervaded by an incomparably strong alcoholic odor. The boy started back with a look of terror. That pale terror was reflected on each man's face, as on a mirror. At the sight of the young stranger they all sprang up with the same gesture, — each instinctively laid his hand upon the pistol that he wore.

Poor Rick understood it all at last. He had stumbled upon a nest of distillers, only too common among these mountains, who were hiding from the officers of the Government, running their still in defiance of the law and eluding the whiskey-tax. He realized that in discovering their stronghold he had learned a secret that was by no means a safe one for him to know. And he was in their power; at their mercy!

" Don't shoot ! " he faltered. " I jes' want ter ax the folkses ter tell me the way ter Birk's Mill."

What would he have given to be on the bleak mountain outside !

One of the men caught him as if anticipating an attempt to run. Two or three, after a low-toned colloquy, took their rifles, and crept cautiously outside to reconnoitre the situation. Rick comprehended their suspicion with new quakings. They imagined that he was a spy, and had been sent among them to discover them plying their forbidden vocation. This threatened a long imprisonment for them. His heart sank as he thought of it ; they would never let him go.

After a time the reconnoitring party came back.

" Nothin' stirrin'," said the leader tersely.

" I misdoubts," muttered another, casting a look of deep suspicion on Rick. " Thar air men out thar, I 'm a-thinkin', hid somewhar."

" They air furder 'n a mile off, ennyhow," returned the first speaker. " We never lef' so much ez a bush 'thout sarchin' of it."

" The off'cers can't find this place no-ways 'thout that thar chap fur a guide," said a third, with a surly nod of his head at Rick.

" We 're safe enough, boys, safe enough ! " cried a stout-built, red-faced, red-bearded man, evidently very drunk, and with a voice that rose into quavering falsetto as he spoke. " This chap can't do nothin'. We hev got him bound hand an' foot. Hyar air the captive of our bow an' spear, boys ! Mighty little captive, though ! hi ! " He tried to point jeeringly at Rick, and forgot what he had intended to do before he could fairly extend his hand. Then his rollicking head sank on his breast, and he began to sing sleepily again.

One of the more sober of the men had extinguished the fire in order that they should not be betrayed by the smoke outside to the revenue officers who might be seeking them. The place, chilly enough at best, was growing bitter cold. The strange subterranean beauty of the surroundings, the limestone wall and arches, scintillating wherever they caught the light; the shadowy, mysterious vaulted roof; the white stalactites that hung down thence to touch the stalagmites as they rose up from the floor, and formed with them endless vistas of stately colonnades, all were oddly incongruous with the drunken, bloated faces of the distillers. Rick could not have put his thought into words, but it seemed to him that when men had degraded themselves like this, even inanimate nature is something higher and nobler. "Sermons in stones" were not far to seek.

He observed that they were making preparations for flight, and once more the fear of what they would do with him clutched at his heart. He was something of a problem to them.

"This hyar cub will go blab," was the first suggestion.

"He will keep mum," said the vocalist, glancing at the boy with a jovially tipsy combination of leer and wink. "Hyar is the persuader!" He rapped sharply on the muzzle of his pistol. "This 'll scotch his wheel."

"Hold yer own jaw, ye drunken 'possum!" retorted another of the group. "Ef ye fire off that pistol in hyar, we'll hev all these hyar rocks"—he pointed at the walls and the long colonnades—"answerin' back an' yelpin' like a pack o' hounds on a hot scent. Ef thar air folks outside, the noise would fotch 'em down on us fur true!"

Rick breathed more freely. The rocks would speak up for him! He could not be harmed with all these tell-tale witnesses at hand. So silent now, but with a latent voice strong enough for the dread of it to save his life!

The man who had put out the fire, who had led the reconnoitring party, who had made all the active preparations for departure, who seemed, in short, to be an executive committee of one,—a long, lazy-looking mountaineer, with a decision of action in startling contrast to his whole aspect,—now took this matter in hand.

"Nothin' easier," he said tersely. "Fill him up. Make him ez drunk ez a fraish b'iled ow*el*. Then lead him to the t'other eend o' the cave, an' blindfold him, an' lug him off five mile in the woods, an' leave him thar. He'll never know what he hev seen nor done."

"That's the dinctum!" cried the red-bearded man, in delighted approval, breaking into a wild, hiccupping laugh, inexpressibly odious to the boy. Rick had an extreme loathing for them all that showed itself with impolitic frankness upon his face. He realized as he had never done before the depths to which strong drink will reduce men. But that the very rocks would cry out upon them, they would have murdered him.

In the preparations for departure all the lights had been extinguished, except a single lantern, and a multitude of shadows had come thronging from the deeper recesses of the cave. In the faint glimmer the figures of the men loomed up, indistinct, gigantic, distorted. They hardly seemed men at all to Rick; rather some evil underground creatures, neither beast nor human.

And he was to be made equally besotted, and even more helpless than they, in order that his senses might be sapped away, and he should remember no story to tell. Perhaps if he had not had before him so vivid an illustration of the malign power that swayed them, he might not have experienced so strong an aversion to it. Now, to be made like them seemed a high price to pay for his life. And there was his promise to his mother! As the long, lank, lazy-looking mountaineer pressed the whiskey upon him, Rick dashed it aside with a gesture so unexpected and vehement that the cracked jug fell to the floor, and was shivered to fragments.

Rick lifted an appealing face to the man, who seized him with a strong grip. "I can't —I won't," the boy cried wildly. "I — I — promised my mother!"

He looked around the circle deprecatingly. He expected first a guffaw and then a blow, and he dreaded the ridicule more than the pain.

But there were neither blows nor ridicule.

They all gazed at him, astounded. Then a change, which Rick hardly comprehended, flitted across the face of the man who had grasped him. The moonshiner turned away abruptly, with a bitter laugh that startled all the echoes.

"*I — I* promised *my* mother, too!" he cried. "It air good that in her grave whar she is she can't know how I hev kep' my word."

And then there was a sudden silence. It seemed to Rick, strangely enough, like the sudden silence that comes after prayer. He was reminded, as one of the men rose at length and the keg on which he had been sitting creaked with the motion, of the creaking benches in the little mountain church when the congregation started from their knees. And had some feeble, groping sinner's prayer filled the silence and the moral darkness!

The "executive committee" promptly recovered himself. But he made no further attempt to force the whiskey upon the boy. Under some whispered instructions which he gave the others, Rick was half-led, half-dragged through immensely long black halls of the cave, while one of the men went before, carrying the feeble lantern. When the first glimmer of daylight appeared in the distance, Rick understood that the cave had an outlet other than the one by which he had entered, and evidently miles distant from it. Thus it was that the distillers were well enabled to baffle the law that sought them.

They stopped here and blindfolded the boy. How far and where they dragged him through the snowy mountain wilderness outside, Rick never knew. He was exhausted when at length they allowed him to pause. As he heard their steps dying away in the distance, he tore the bandage from his eyes, and found that they had left him in the midst of the wagon road to make his way to Birk's Mill as best he might. When he reached it, the wintry sun was low in the western sky, and the very bones of the " pea-fow*el* " were picked.

On the whole, it seemed a sorry Christmas

Day, as Rick could not know then — indeed, he never knew — what good results it brought forth. For among those who took the benefit of the " amnesty " extended by the Government to the moonshiners of this region, on condition that they discontinue illicit distilling for the future, was a certain long, lank, lazy-looking mountaineer, who suddenly became sober and steady and a law-abiding citizen. He had been reminded, this Christmas Day, of a broken promise to a dead mother, and this by the unflinching moral courage of a mere boy in a moment of mortal peril. Such wise, sweet, uncovenanted uses has duty, blessing alike the unconscious exemplar and him who profits by the example.

www.ingramcontent.com/pod-product-compliance
Lightning Source LLC
Chambersburg PA
CBHW020340030726
47496CB00007B/1958